PRAISE FO

BLUEPRINTS FOR A BARBED-WIRE CANOE

'Wayne Macauley has the soul of a poet and his surreal novella is stunningly written...It is a satire of exquisite poise and confidence...If more Australian literature was of this calibre, we'd be laughing.' *Age*

'A salutary fable about the horrors awaiting our disaffected modern citizenry...lasting visual images and resonant symbolism.' *Sydney Morning Herald*

'Bewitching...ethereal...hallucinatory...In an era when many Australian novelists are playing it safe...Wayne Macauley is an ambitious talent worth watching.' *Wet Ink*

'Tapping the hidden heart of a different Australia... this is original Australian writing at its best.' *Courier-Mail*

'Like falling into a bale of barbed wire in the dark and fighting to get out till morning. The more I struggled, the more it got under my skin.' *Bulletin*

Wayne Macauley has published three novels, most recently *The Cook*, and the short fiction collection *Other Stories*. He lives in Melbourne.

waynemacauley.com

BLUEPRINTS FOR A BARBED-WIRE CANOE

WAYNE MACAULEY

TEXT PUBLISHING MELBOURNE AUSTRALIA

textpublishing.com.au

The Text Publishing Company
Swann House
22 William Street
Melbourne Victoria 3000
Australia

First published by Black Pepper, Melbourne Australia, 2004
This edition published by The Text Publishing Company, 2012

Cover design by WH Chong
Page design by Text
Printed and bound in Australia by Griffin Press

Epigraph from *The Lament for Ur*, Thorkild Jacobsen (trans.), *The Harps That Once...*, Yale University Press (1987)

National Library of Australia Cataloguing-in-Publication entry:
Author: Macauley, Wayne.
Title: Blueprints for a barbed-wire canoe / Wayne Macauley.
ISBN: 9781922079114 (pbk.)
ISBN: 9781921961342 (ebook)
Dewey Number: A823.3

The paper this book is printed on is certified against the Forest Stewardship Council® Standards. Griffin Press holds FSC chain of custody certification SGS-COC-005088. FSC promotes environmentally responsible, socially beneficial and economically viable management of the world's forests.

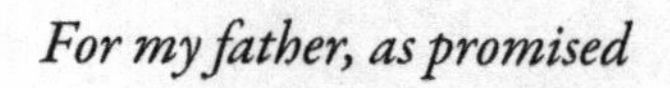

For my father, as promised

Brickwork of Ur, bitter is the wail,
The wail set up for you!
...
O my flooded, washed away,
brickwork of Ur!

FROM AN ANCIENT SUMERIAN POEM

one

It had rained for three days solid, in some places the creek had already burst its banks; she'd waited for nightfall, a night with no moon. No-one can say how spectacularly unsuccessful the launching was; no-one was there on that dark night to bear witness. Though the remnants of the canoe were found the following day wrapped crazily around an overhanging branch almost a kilometre down-stream, there is little point speculating on how much of the journey was made on the surface, as hoped, and how much of it tumbling in the putrid waters beneath. The body itself outdistanced the canoe by a kilometre and a half and was recovered two days later wedged between the root of a tree and the grey mud of the bank. It wore, ridiculously, the uniform prescribed: the rabbit-skin hat still held in place by a chin strap, the jacket still neatly buttoned.

I was asked into town to sign some papers and I drove there dazed and shaken. Patterson himself seemed genuinely upset. It was, we both knew, a strange and futile end to a strange and futile saga. Little was said, little could be said; I saw the body, identified her as Jodie and drove back home with the image of her blood-drained face and quiet closed-forever eyes before me.

The rain wouldn't stop, it came down in endless thin silver ropes, pelting the roof and bursting out of the gutters; it was washing everything, washing everything clean, the whole sad sorry story, across the paddocks and ruins, from trickles to rivulets to the creek into the far-off sea. That night, as I sat down at my table and prepared to break the news to Michael, I knew, at last, that my days here were done.

Michael! Mad, bad, cockeyed Michael! That it should all come to this! All the twisted lines of our journey, the scratches, the cuts, the bruises, were marked on her face. But serene, so serene, ghost-white and pure. Michael! Oh, Michael! That it should all come to this!

I loaded the car up with beer from the pub in town and pulled the table up that night to within arm's reach of the fridge. Empty cans littered the table, the rain drummed hard on the roof. Hours passed; they could have been years. I couldn't write to Michael, there were no words to fix the image, wrap it in sympathy and carry it safely to him: six screwed-up pieces of paper lay strewn across the floor. I raised myself unsteadily from the table, stood at the back door and looked out at the rain. It had already washed the gravel from the path leading down the back to the creek and the paddocks beyond lay shrouded in darkness and damp. She'd have passed by here, just down there at the end of the path, beyond the murky shaft of light, where I could hear the sound of the boiling, rushing water even now. Was she standing, head held high as instructed, or already tumbling, groping, lost? I'd have been sleeping, the rain on the roof. And she passed by softly: I couldn't have heard.

I took up the lamp, put on my coat, and walked out into the rain. I made my way down North Court and trudged to the top of the mountain of rubble that overlooked the square. It was a lake now, a low lake of muddy water in which a few persistent gorse bushes still stood. Nothing to suggest the summer evenings of soft orange light, the clinking of glasses and the hubbub of talk; those long magical evenings now a lifetime away. Grey sky, grey mud, grey water, drenched by an unending rain.

I walked down the eastern side of the hill towards the few houses that still stood, miraculously, north-east of the square. My boots were caked with mud, my steps were leaden. Thick weeds, gorse and thistle had long ago claimed the streets; they slapped at my thighs, tore at my flesh and wet my trousers through.

I walked into the lounge room of an empty house; it reeked of dogs, bird droppings and damp. A bird flew out the window, leaving the echo of its flapping in the room. I remembered Michael, and our meeting in the abandoned house on West Court all those years ago. Flies buzzed in zigzag patterns around the broken light fitting and the dogs stretched and yawned on the burnt-brown lawn. That summer was the worst: the paddocks around us were dead grass and dust; the streets melted, the gardens withered, a heat shimmer wobbled and distorted everything in the middle distance and beyond. Days on end spent waiting for night, nights on end spent dreading the days, we cowed beneath an open sky, hugging the walls and shadows, listening with one ear cocked to the distant rumblings whose source we could still not name. He was her father, I was in love with her, all my words were servant to these truths.

I trudged back home, my boots and the shoulders of my coat soaked through, and lit a fire in the grate. Steam rose from the boots on the hearth and the coat flung over the chair: it hung below the ceiling like a cloud threatening rain. Rain, rain, everywhere the rain. It battered the roof and dripped with an insistent rhythm into the saucepans. I sat at the table and gazed again at the objects assembled there: a piece of glass from a broken beer bottle, a chipped house brick, a charred rabbit bone. I arranged and rearranged them on the table before me, imploring them to tell a story, to reconstitute themselves into a whole. But they remained stubbornly themselves: inert, mute, adrift. So are these few relics all that I have salvaged from the ruins of those years? Small things, absurd, earth-encrusted things. Had I not come back to dig them out they would still be sleeping peacefully where they should be, in the all-forgiving earth.

Later that night I awoke in the chair; the fire was cold, a heavy pounding in my head. I'd woken with her image before me again, the cold white face, the matted hair, her stomach so flat that it almost looked shrunken; the great fertile hump she'd been carrying, gone. I caught Patterson's eye; he half-shrugged. The baby hadn't been found.

With that image before me I couldn't sleep, and I spent the next hour or more outside gathering up old bricks and rubble, anything I could find, to make a low dyke across the backyard, which I hoped would save me at least until morning. The creek down there was spreading now; bits of rubbish floated past and the stench was unbearable. Across the paddocks the puddles had swollen into lakes, the labyrinth of rabbit warrens flooded; the rain lashed the dead grasses unabating. I lit the fire again and pulled the blanket tight around me, so many things clawing at my head. The tangled barbed wire and splintered wood wrapped around a tree; Jodie, growing ever-flatter in my mind, a cigarette paper laid out on a slab, white and so insubstantial that a mere puff of breath might blow her away; the tiny blue-grey bundle of flesh tumbling in the filthy waters, God knows, still tumbling now past Konagaderra, Wildwood, Bulla to the bay and on into the soundless sea.

Yes, I came back; only fools do that, to live among these ruins in a slapped-up shack of leftovers. And for my foolishness I've become the only witness to the final act, last spectator in an empty theatre, last left squinting when the lights come on, the only one to take the final image out into the street. You're the only one of the old group we could find, said Patterson, as if for that I should be pitied. And probably I should.

The earth can only take so much rain and as the night wore on I felt it gulping ever-closer to its limit. The bridge was gone, my car was drowned; I was on an island surrounded by a sea of dirty water. I arranged the objects on my table again. I emptied the saucepans and mopped the floor. I couldn't sleep. I opened a can, lit the lamp, pulled the table up by the fire and wrote.

two

It was a mistake from the first. In the early days a much talked about and heralded mistake but a mistake nonetheless. I was a victim of the publicity, I can't pretend otherwise. I was, if anything, its greatest victim, harbouring to the very end my belief that everything would, despite the setbacks, soon or at least one day all work out as planned.

The country was changing, the population exploding; we were no longer a few fly specks on a huge uncluttered map. Our cities were becoming enormous, unsightly and ever-expanding blotches; my own, my birthplace, south of here, Melbourne, the most unsightly and expanding of all. So it didn't take much for some new upstart town planners, the ink hardly dry on their diplomas, to convince the civic authorities that a new approach to urban planning was needed. It was all very well to be encouraging new housing development in the outer suburbs to lessen the pressure on the city's resources, but, they argued, there was really no point in simply tacking one new development onto the back fence, as it were, of the one just completed; far from encouraging moves away from the city this was simply grafting the new population onto it. We must, they said, look 'further out'.

This reasoning was all very well, and there was a good deal of sense in it. But, with the benefit of hindsight, they made two fundamental mistakes. First, in their great enthusiasm, they looked *too far out*, and second, they looked too far out *in the wrong direction*.

Using perhaps no more than a slide rule and the logic of their fanciful theories, they fixed on a point over fifty kilometres north of the city to establish the first 'new estate'. It mattered little to them in what kind of landscape this estate stood: those who ended up living there were always convinced that the whole thing had been planned and approved on the basis of a red pin stuck on a wall map in some obscure city office. But the north it was: past the tired potholed suburbs on the city fringe and the brick veneer additions of recent years, past the For Lease factories with bare asphalt carparks marked out in white, the used car lots, the wrecking yards, past the miserable market garden plots full of cabbage gone to seed and on through the flat and never-changing expanse of paddocks, dead trees, broken barbed-wire fences, bored cows, hang-gutted horses, and here and there the rusted shell of an abandoned car. Forty hectares of overworked and abandoned farmland, half encircled by a small creek with steep-sided banks, pockmarked with rabbit holes and decorated by gorse and Scotch thistle: this was the spot to which the surveyors were sent armed with their mysterious three-legged instruments, weaving in and out of the gorse bushes with tape measures in their hands and hammering in their orange marker pegs in a strange and almost incomprehensible array of patterns.

The estate was built in record time and the official opening was attended by many dignitaries, the most important of whom, the Premier no less, unveiled the small bronze plaque that up until the destruction still stood on the grass plantation in the centre of the square. It was all a cause for great civic pride at the time and those of us who were there, the first residents, guinea pigs if you like, felt that we were taking part in an event of great national importance. Speeches were made, a large marquee covered the square, and beer, wine and savouries were served. I hope, said the Premier, one hand on the podium to prevent his speech being carried off by the wind, that this will become the model of things to come.

And yes, despite its questionable location and the hurry to completion, despite everything that has happened since, the estate was a model of the new planning ideas at the time and was, in its way, absolutely unique. It was designed as a kind of self-contained village: a main square in the centre surrounded by shops, a bank, a post office and so on, with four streets radiating out from this square to each point of the compass. Each of these four streets then crossed a ring road some forty metres out from the square with all except one terminating on the other side in three bubble-shaped culs-de-sac or courts. The fourth or eastbound street crossed the ring road and continued on for little over a kilometre until it met up with the main highway to the city—the only access, by road, to the estate. Four further culs-de-sac or courts branched off from the ring road, making seven in all.

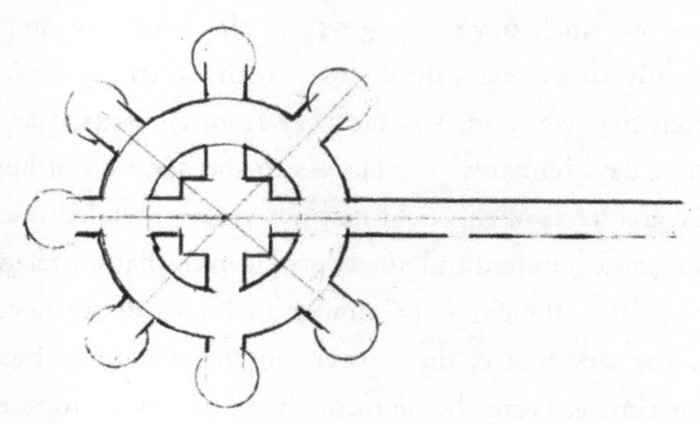

So that the whole thing resembled, if seen from the air and with a touch of imagination, the great wheel of an old sailing ship bound for exotic new lands. The four streets and seven courts were named according to their corresponding positions on the compass; North Street, East Street, North Court, North-East Court, etc...And they all, including the ring road, were lined with houses—two hundred and twenty in all and all identical in design: three bedroom solid brick with front yard, backyard, driveway and garage. On the basis of four and a half persons per household, the designers had calculated on a population of nine hundred and ninety people.

It was, to anyone's way of seeing things, an extraordinary achievement. Out of the bare inhospitable paddocks a new village had arisen: neat, clean and impeccably ordered, far from the unkempt sprawl of the city. There was one small town a long way to the south-east and a slightly larger one a little closer to the north, but aside from that we seemed as far away from civilisation as is these days humanly possible. As to the question of how the architects of this bold new adventure intended resettling nine hundred and ninety people in the flat wasteland over fifty kilometres (or almost an hour's drive) north of the city centre, the answer, on the surface at least, was simple. From the moment the project was proposed there was, hand in hand with it, the further proposal of constructing an enormous six-lane freeway from the city fringe to just over the fifty kilometre mark. Obviously, without this hand-in-hand proposal, well advertised as a *fait accompli*, no-one would ever have moved to the estate in the first place: aside from those who, counting on a population sufficient to sustain them, intended setting up businesses there, it was obvious that the remaining majority would have to commute to the city for work. The freeway proposal promised to reduce a commuting time of almost an hour to a little under half that; a significant reduction. Two further carrots were dangled, and not unimportant ones either. All those who lived on the estate were to be issued with 'residency cards', proving they lived there and allowing them on production of their card to buy petrol at the petrol station that was to be built on the eastern access road at *half the usual price*. (The residency cards were in fact issued; the phantom petrol station is another story.) In other words, you could drive from the estate to the city and back every day and still come out with a weekly petrol bill no worse and in some cases even better than before. The final carrot, and the most important for many, was a case of economics in its crudest form. The estate was government-subsidised and all the houses available there cost on average one third less than a house of similar size and design as the many to be found on the suburban fringe. For those with a dream of owning their own home but without the means to do so, this was an enormous incentive to make the long journey north.

A hundred and twenty-six official residents attended the opening gala that day (though we still didn't have our residency cards, on that day we nevertheless felt official), and though a hundred and twenty-six is a long way from nine hundred and ninety it did nothing to dampen the enthusiasm. They were an odd assortment of people: young married couples, new immigrant families, older folk who had come to escape the city and slowly count out the days to their retirement, and, as to be expected, a small number of more established families from the towns further north (farmers mostly) who, with an eye to the discount petrol, had in addition made no small profit on the sale of their own houses against the much cheaper purchase of an estate one. There was no-one there that day who couldn't fail to feel a sense of importance, of being part of a great experiment, the success of which, to most people's minds, was already assured. But hardly had the marquee and bunting been taken down than the first grumblings began.

There were problems with the sewage: the first real indication of the haste with which, especially in the final stages, the estate had been built and what effect this had on the workers' attention to detail. The sewage pipes were connected to each house, to be sure, and these pipes linked to the main line which was to carry the effluent away. But further to that no plans were made and, as was later found, the main line simply stopped about twenty metres beyond North-East Court and discharged its contents there. At this point, on the northern fringe of the estate, a small creek passes in an east-west direction before turning south towards the sea—usually drying to a trickle in summer but often flooded in winter—and it's into this creek that the sewage found its way. (It is an even greater cause for disbelief to remember that, at the time, there was a plan to dam this creek at a point a little west of the estate, excavate a large area east of this dam and so create a lake that was to become the central feature of a five-hectare recreational park.) The creek began to stink, so much so that those who had bought houses on the northern edge (and they were not a few, having heard and believed the story of the park) soon applied to swap them for houses on the other side of the estate. The northern sector became deserted. The petrol station, despite the endless promises, was and remained no more than a large concrete slab that had been hastily poured one afternoon a week or so after the opening. Four square metal plates with four rusting bolts in each were the only evidence left that they ever had any intention of returning to erect the structure. Finally, as if to rub salt into our wounds, we soon found that not a single telephone on the estate worked: every phone was dead.

With the odour of sewage wafting through our doors and windows whenever the breeze was from the north and with the realisation that the offer of discount petrol had been no more than an empty promise, many people quickly made plans to get out. For Sale signs went up in the front yards of a number of houses but the grass grew thick around them. Rumours of the estate's problems had already reached back to the city and no-one wanted to buy. A few households took down the signs and decided, with a certain fatalism that marked the period to follow, to stay; others, desperate to get out at any cost, eventually sold their houses back to the government at a fraction of the price they'd paid for them. In this way we lost (I'm speaking of the first twelve months here) eight families in all: those that remained had quickly established themselves in the southern part of the estate, as far away as possible from the creek. The northern part quickly fell into neglect; wild grass, gorse and thistle took over and grew to chest height in the yards and gardens. Weeds forced their way up through and widened the cracks in the footpaths and streets. With the combined weight of sometimes ten or twenty birds' nests the eaves on the houses began to sag and collapse. And, in the case of those houses on the very northern edge, the combined forces of the first winter's rains, a swollen creek and a small moving sea of effluent soon served to undermine the foundations. The houses themselves began to sag and crack—in one case a whole front wall falling over onto the lawn, exposing an empty lounge room with the paint already flaking from the walls and the half-rotted body of an old stray dog inside.

By the end of the second year (Inauguration Day was marked by a small protest in the square) many more people had left, but a relative handful, some fifty in all, had decided to stay. Though no-one believed in the petrol station any more, the freeway was still a hard dream to give up. As the greater part of the estate began to fall apart around us, the remaining population—concentrated around and to the south of the square—were drawn together all the more tightly. We believed, despite the unfinished works and unfulfilled promises, that the freeway would come: it was hard for us to believe how it could not, given that the whole rationale of the estate's existence was based on the very fact of its coming. It was only a matter of waiting, we told ourselves, and of making the best of it in the meantime.

But such faith was misguided: by the end of the third year, still without a freeway and with the population now reduced to a mere twenty-seven adults, five children and an uncountable number of dogs and cats, the real situation became clear. The original planners *had* made a mistake: they'd built an estate over fifty kilometres north of the city but the fact was that in the intervening years it had become clear to everyone that the north was not the place to be. Under the influence of various private property developers who, soon after the declared government backing of a northward expansion, had wisely bought up vast tracts of land on the much more lush and hospitable eastern belt, the suburbs had begun to march unstoppably in that direction. Housing was cheap, one estate was quickly grafted onto the next to form whole new suburbs, families moved there by the thousands, new business and employment opportunities flourished and before long the expansion had moved so far out that the idea of building a freeway north at the expense of the much more obvious needs of those in the east became, for those originally responsible for our estate, unsustainable. The northern freeway was 'temporarily delayed' (as if it had not been delayed already) and all the money, equipment and manpower was immediately transferred to the construction of a new eastern freeway, to be completed with all possible haste.

The north was suddenly and quite brutally forgotten. All those previously responsible for the estate's planning and construction quickly wiped their hands of it and turned their eyes to the east. The estate fell back in on itself, more isolated than ever. House prices fell dramatically again (they were now hardly worth more than the dry earth they stood on) and, however much they may have wanted to get out, few people could afford to sell at such a loss. We protested, of course, and the government, no doubt driven by guilt, responded to our protests with the payment of a small monthly subsidy to those hardy residents who had decided to stay. Rest assured, they said, the freeway will come—but the wait may be a long one and we should not be made to suffer in the meantime. Finally, and a little ridiculously, as if to expunge any remaining guilt, a telephone box for which no coins were needed suddenly appeared overnight in the square.

The original dream was shattered, all but the deluded had fled, and in the end six three-bedroom solid brick homes on South Street and one, incongruously, on the edge of North Court, were occupied by one person each.

So this was the estate, the *Outer Suburban Village Development Complex*, as the sign on the access road called it, a now dead and forgotten place, testament for any visitor who may chance upon it—and they, believe me, were few—to some now very anonymous architect's grand but misguided vision. We gathered in the square of an evening to drink and talk (it was summer when the last rat jumped ship and left us seven to sink or swim) and at that hour, as the heat of the day began to subside—and the heat out there in the height of summer was almost unbearable—the estate did for a time begin to resemble as closely as it ever might the village the original planners had in mind. Ignore the empty and tumbledown houses, the gardens of wild grass and gorse, pass over the stench from the creek and the streets and footpaths riven with cracks, and you might almost see the faint stirrings of a new community being born.

Around us on the square the shops remained empty and ghost-infested, white masking tape crosses still stuck to their windows. Weeds crept up through the cracks at our feet, starlings flew home to roost under the supermarket awning. Far, far away you could hear the tortured bellowing of a cow. On the grass plantation in the centre of the square, where the bronze plaque still stood as a somewhat incongruous reminder of an old dream long faded, a motley assortment of dogs and cats gathered to sniff, gambol and doze. The evenings fell slowly, casting long shadows across the square, and, clear as we were of the city lights, night revealed above us a magical cupola of stars.

three

All that, all talk of that, all that hard imagining of things so far away and long gone, leaves me empty and cold. It's as if I had invented it all, in order to speak of other things. But it happened, I was there, and the more I look back on it the more I come to believe that the long stretch of time up to those evenings I've described, the history of the estate per se, was in fact mere prehistory and that that moment, somewhere there, under the stars, was the real beginning. But that's the trouble. It was always the beginning, has always been and probably always will be. Even now, don't I sometimes lie in my bed at night and dream of a new estate rising from the ruins? Don't I say to myself, Bram, take heart, keep faith, this may merely be the prelude of greater things to come? But then who am I to speak at all, to pretend to give a description of something that is still, to this day, beyond even my comprehension? I'm a nobody really, and should shut my mouth.

I came to the estate, alone and untroubled by my aloneness, with no greater ambition than to set up a small local paper—*The Voice*—which, I had calculated, by selling to nine hundred and ninety residents at fifty cents a copy, would have not only recouped its costs but also given me a modest annual income. That was enough, I wanted no more. And in the early days a good few copies of *The Voice* did indeed run off the press that I had installed in my spare room and were sold through the newsagent's in the square and my position as writer, editor and publisher did indeed afford me a certain standing in the community at the time, given that most of its pages were filled with accusatory articles and bombastic editorials about the one thing that was concerning us most: namely that we had been conned, and were now destined, it seemed, to end our days living in little more than a well-designed slum. And if my aforementioned calculations ended up falling a good deal short of the mark (a hundred and twenty-six official residents is a long way from nine hundred and ninety, and seven a long way further than that) and I was eventually forced to survive on my small amount of savings and the government's monthly subsidy, still, my standing in the community was not lessened as a result and in some ways even strengthened (I could be indignant from personal experience now) and my opinions were still valued, indeed, often worshipped. But still, *what does that qualify me for in the end*? Perhaps this: to merely say that no description of the estate, no matter how scrupulous, could ever hope to be the true history itself. I am more qualified than most to set the record straight—and I'm sure my old friends and neighbours would agree—but the burden of truth is a heavy one that I'm often unable to bear.

Out in the east the houses sprouted like mushrooms and marched on through the orchards and bush. Streets were filled with playing children, backyards filled with barbecues and beer, shopping centres on Friday evenings were a swirling joyous mass of humanity. It might have been another world, so far away was it from our small forgotten outpost in the north. There they grew shrubs and trees, green as emeralds in the sunlight, and walked or rode through parks and playing fields with sweet grass-smelling thoughts in their heads. (I don't begrudge them their freeway and never have, they were obviously more deserving of it than us, but what sometimes irks me is that they took it for granted, as an almost inalienable right, not daring to consider that it was in fact ours to begin with and had without warning been cruelly snatched from us.) We by contrast lived like dry stones scattered under an unforgiving sky; we had no mighty river of a freeway to irrigate us, to give us cars and life. We had to make the best of what we had, hunker down, and find some way of sustaining this precarious, perhaps ridiculous, existence.

We were an odd group, those seven residents who had each for their own reasons decided to stay, and I sometimes wonder how we all got on as well as we did for so long. Loners basically, of one sort or another, who had each wanted only to be an anonymous one among a population of a thousand but who were now the only residents left and the estate's entire reason for being. It was Vito who eventually broke the ice. A wiry old Italian with a moustachioed smile whose leftish ideas had apparently got him into some trouble during the war (this at least was how he explained the missing finger), he had for some time been growing vegetables in his backyard. I waved to him occasionally, as he sat on his front porch of an evening. But, despite the undoubted skill of this loveable man, the soil in his backyard proved to be hard and unyielding. He produced a crop, and a decent crop too, enough in a good year to feed himself and occasionally leave a cabbage, a pumpkin or a bunch of carrots anonymously on our doorsteps, but they nowhere near approached the quality of the remembered vegetables of his youth. Then I saw him one day, out on a paddock south of the creek, just beyond

North-East Court, with his shirt off and a shovel in his hand. He worked for weeks, alone, damming up the creek and diverting the effluent from the main sewage line off into a series of irrigation channels and throwing up beds of earth. He planted his seedlings out in rows and spent each day out on the paddock that spring lovingly tending to them. The following summer the crop came on: beans the size of zucchinis and zucchinis the size of melons. Late that summer Vito drove his first load of produce into town and returned to the estate that afternoon with an onion sack full of cash. This is for everyone, he said, as he stood on my doorstep: we can use it to make repairs and so on and keep everything looking good. I invited him inside and counted the money onto the table.

That evening I wrote and printed a small leaflet that I posted the following morning in the square. It said, in effect, that on Vito's initiative a petty cash account had now been formed which I had been entrusted with administering; anyone who for whatever reason needed money to tide them over from one week to the next need only apply in person for a small handout to be given, and if anyone, following Vito's example, wished in their own way to contribute to this fund, then this too would obviously be welcomed. I further suggested that we now pool our monthly subsidies into a joint account in the bank in town, keep them there, and use the annual interest for any additional unforeseen costs.

My leaflet had the desired effect and Vito's spirit of enterprise soon became infectious. Nanna (we only ever knew her as Nanna), who had originally come to the estate to set up a flower shop on the square and keep herself busy in her retirement but who had never had more than a handful of customers darken her doorstep, now walked down the access road to the highway every weekend with a bucket of flowers and a foldaway chair and came back every evening with a jam jar full of coins. Craig the squatter, a young man in his early twenties who had taken up residence in one of the empty houses in South Street some time in the second year and who had lived there unchallenged ever since, began scavenging in the deserted houses for whatever he could sell to the second-hand dealer in town—door handles, tap fittings, stoves, carpets—and every Friday at five delivered the profits from these transactions to me in a white plastic bag. Each week Dave added two dozen bottles of his home-brewed beer to Vito's produce and in a fit of benevolence Slug the real estate agent suddenly offered to buy us a trailer, a pump and a generator with no strings attached. Michael (mad Michael!) began shouldering his gun every morning at dawn and heading out on the paddocks to shoot rabbits, returning at lunchtime with perhaps a dozen strung on a coathanger at his waist: we took one each if we wanted, the rest went into town with the vegetables and were sold to the butcher there.

An economy had been born—though, true, a strange one—with me as honorary if somewhat reluctant treasurer. Later that year, and by mutual agreement, all the cars on the estate except Vito's station wagon were communally sold (what need had we of cars, we who had no freeway?) and this money was in turn added to the fund that I now kept in a shoebox in the bottom of my cupboard. We, more than anyone, were aware of our own ridiculousness—no-one who lived through that time could have failed to have a sense of humour—but nor could we ignore that small sense of belonging, of having made the best of a bad situation.

The seasons began to assume a pattern, unimaginable in the early days when our preoccupations were more with freeways, petrol subsidies and sewage lines than the mysteries of sky and earth. After Vito's paddock was flooded in winter and the first days of spring broke clear and blue, the beds were prepared and the planting begun. True, the majority of us would barely have glanced at the foul-smelling four hectares of market garden through the long months of winter and might well have forgotten it was there, but come summer and the harvest it was the centre of our lives. Every morning Vito roused us from our beds with a blast on the horn, every evening the old station wagon came back from town with its sackful of cash and bootful of supplies, all washed down with bottle after bottle from Dave's new batch of beer.

The brewery had begun as a hobby, a small enterprise in the back corner of his garage; he'd perfected the art long before coming to the estate—he was a man well into his sixties—and had gained quite a reputation, as he always insisted on telling us, in the street where he used to live. He always made more than he could drink himself and would hand out bottles to his neighbours at Christmas wrapped in cellophane and tied with a bow. He'd lost his wife many years before and where under these circumstances many would have turned to their roses or orchids, Dave turned ever more passionately to the perfection of his brew. It was a wheat beer, brewed in the bottle, high in sugar content and rich with the sweet taste of fermentation. Occasionally in the silence of the night the sound of an exploding bottle could be heard echoing beneath the garage roof and rattling the roller door. Though the beer was Dave's it was Slug's idea to set up the bar (what an enterprising mind that man had!) and it was he who provided the premises.

Slug was a real estate agent and had opened an office on the square on the western corner of North Street. As the one agent on the estate he was obviously preparing himself to make a killing (he originally employed an assistant and two secretaries, who waited patiently each day behind their desks for the avalanche of enquiries to begin) but of all the original inhabitants he was undoubtedly the greatest victim. He dealt with a good few sales for a while, it's true, but sales back to the government that earned him such a small commission that it could barely cover his overheads. And after the announcement of the freeway's 'delay' he knew better than anyone that his days as a real estate agent were numbered. Again, as for everyone, it's hard to say why he stayed. He was a man in his early fifties, divorced, without children, and his corpulence above all testified to his love of the dollar and the many and varied ways to relieve himself of it. But perhaps that's the point; the collapse of his business produced just the crisis he'd needed to kiss that old life goodbye and seek pleasure and fulfilment in the simpler things. One of these things was Dave's beer and they became great drinking partners and friends. But his business acumen hadn't entirely left him and shortly after the last house was sold—the young couple watched weeping on the lawn as their furniture was loaded up and driven away—he transformed his office into the bar-cum-café that had perhaps been his secret dream all along. At first the only customers were Dave and Slug themselves, and they sat together at a table outside drinking themselves into a stupor through the eventless afternoons. But one by one, and with little else to do, the other residents began to stop by occasionally to share a bottle with them. And so for the others, what started out as a casual way of killing an hour or two soon became a habit, and often by the time evening fell you were just as likely to find the whole population of the estate gathered there under the awning on the corner of North Street and the square.

A motley collection of ill-matched tables and chairs was hastily put together and arranged out on the footpath. Three fridges that had been left behind by owners too tired and beaten to bother moving them were collected from the houses where they had been gathering dust and installed in a row out the back. A sign went up in the window—*Slug's*—and there, at any time of the day, you could savour the sweet taste of Dave's home-brewed beer poured fresh from the bottle by the brewer himself. It wasn't a grand money-making exercise by any means but Slug wasn't in it for that. A great weight had lifted from him and he was now content to pass the day drinking quietly with his new business partner and in the evening to entertain the customers gathered beneath the awning with stories of his past excesses.

If I can trace back through the labyrinthine history of the estate to a place and time of happy memories it would be a summer evening such as that, with the harvest in and the cash box full, at a table on the corner of North Street with a cold glass of Dave's home brew. A string of lights were hung from the awning to the nearby power pole and the tables and chairs were pushed off the footpath into the square. Slug and Nanna prepared a feast, laid out on a trestle table under the stars, while Dave, in ill-fitting dinner jacket and bow-tie, moved among us with a tray and bottle balanced precariously on the fingers of one hand. The effigy was dressed in its suit and tie, the cardboard briefcase pinned to its hand, and we watched clapping and cheering as Slug put the match to it and the square was filled with a blaze of orange light. Finally, some time after midnight and an hour's baiting, Craig the squatter locked himself in the phone box and, using his half-remembered schoolboy French, dialled a random number in Paris, France, and asked the voice at the other end for directions to the Louvre. All was drunkenness, foolishness, frivolity: clinking bottles, breaking glasses, laughing, shouting; a cacophony of noise under a still, solid sky. At some ungodly hour we staggered back to our respective homes, the six others across the square to South Street, I the longer journey north with a pack of dogs sniffing at my heels. Daytime passed in a slow, quiet, torporific haze; dogs dozed in whatever shade they could find, out on the paddock a humid concoction of sewage-drenched soil and rotting vegetables rose and hung, invisible, over the ground. The creek dried up, tar bubbled in the streets, two hundred and twenty houses shifted, sighed and groaned.

four

Outer Suburban Village Development Complex, the sign on the access road had read, but over the years all but the letters *ur* from *Suburban* had either fallen off or been souvenired by the vandals. In time to come we would take this name—*ur*, a kind of laconic mumble—as our own and keep it as our own private joke, but either way, both then and later, the name remained hidden from everyone but us. We had never appeared on a map under any name, old or new; the cartographers had barely begun to sketch us in before they were forced to erase us again. The dilapidated sign out on the access road was all we had to call attention to our existence, and rare now, if ever, were the times when foreign eyes fell upon it. Occasionally, on a weekend stroll, one of us might see a car pull up out on the access road and a poorly dressed family stand gazing for a while at the strange collection of houses in front of them. But if they had come to consider the idea of moving into the estate then the idea quickly deserted them. The family dog that had scampered down to the ring road corner to sniff the tails of the others who gathered there to greet it was quickly whistled back and leashed, and the family got in and drove away, carrying with them the first chapter of the story they would tell to other poorly dressed families back in the city, a story that would end with the words: No, don't bother, we've seen it and it stinks.

It did stink. Though the sewage produced by a mere seven individuals may be rightly considered a trifle, it was more than enough to infect the slow-moving creek and the market garden with a rich rotting smell that often and particularly in summer hung over the northern part of *ur* like a poisonous cloud. It was a smell all too familiar to me. For reasons I am still hard-pressed to explain, I had remained in my house on the edge of North Court and continued to live there, despite the stink, the sinking foundations and the cracks in the walls, through almost all the years of the estate's existence. Of course, like many others, I had originally bought the house on the strength of the recreation park rumour. But unlike the others I had stayed on after the sewage problem first became apparent and never seriously entertained any thoughts of moving.

Bram from the Far North they called me, and, because of my loyalty to my original dwelling, despite the deterioration around, I suppose I was considered something of an eccentric. I spent most days at my kitchen table, working on some new article or other for *The Voice*, which I still brought out intermittently and for free, or going over the accounts of the fund for which I'd now become official trustee. What I wrote was no longer journalism as such and I'm not even sure, now, how to define it, but my neighbours always waited anxiously for the next issue to appear and were full of praise for its contents when it did. Perhaps they were humouring me, but I was happy to be humoured. And certainly in the height of summer, with the midday heat and the smell from the creek making life outside unbearable, I was content to spend what time I could inside and rarely ventured out until evening.

It was one such evening, towards the end of the first summer harvest, in fact, when, taking my usual stroll around the ring road, stick in hand to ward off the dogs, I turned into South Street on my way back home and heard strange noises—sawing and hammering—coming from Michael's garage. The garage door was open and a shaft of light fell onto the driveway. I could see him inside, de-nailing an old piece of timber. What are you making?

I asked—a question I've since come to believe I should never have asked at all. Michael turned and looked over his shoulder, then turned to his piece of timber again. Nothing, he said. I stepped inside. I've noticed you've been collecting the old barbed wire and bits of timber from the farms around here, I said: I wonder if I could ask you a favour? Michael stopped working. The rabbits have been getting into Vito's garden, I said, and eating the new plants. I was suggesting to him that some kind of fence might be the solution. You seem to know a bit about both—rabbits, I mean, and fences. Michael smiled, the creases tightening in the corners of his eyes. He must have been about fifty-odd, with the wiry frame and leathery skin of someone who has spent most of his life outdoors. But what distinguished him above all was the right eye: something was wrong with it, its gaze skewed sideways and always gave you the disconcerting impression that he was not only looking at you but also at someone over your shoulder. And, as if by way of compensation, his left eye fixed you in a fiery stare that could have burnt holes in concrete. I'm sure you've got other plans for the materials you've got here, I said, but I'd be happy to help you collect some more from the paddocks and give you a hand to build it. Michael went to the fridge in the corner of the garage and took out a bottle of Dave's home brew. He took off the cap and poured two glasses. I was a fencing contractor, he said, handing me a glass: I don't think a vegetable patch would present too many problems for me.

We drank and talked then, well into the night; I never made it back to Slug's for my nightcap. The enigma of Michael was penetrated to some extent, though never completely—it still never has. He'd come from a country town in the west where he'd lived with his wife and teenage daughter, building and fixing fences on the surrounding farms and making a reasonable living out of it. But one day at work he tensioned a piece of barbed wire one millimetre too far; it snapped, and took a piece of Michael's right eye with it as it passed. He was unable to work for almost a year, and the constant friction that had distinguished the relationship between him and his wife finally came to a head. She left him, taking with her their only daughter. The eye eventually healed, enough to give him partial, though badly skewed, vision; he tried to renew his old contracts with the surrounding properties but none of the farmers wanted to have their fences built by a man with only one accurate eye. So he moved to the city, took a night-shift job in a paint factory, spent what little money he earned on drink and the spare time he had left trying to find his wife and daughter. The wife he never found and never would, the daughter he eventually tracked down to a share house in a cheap and ugly suburb, living on nothing and going to the dogs. He took her in with him but had no sooner done so than he lost his factory job, got into a fight with his landlord and was forced out onto the street. The daughter left him again and lived (as hearsay had it) a dissolute life of drink, drugs, arguments and abortions while Michael wandered the uninspiring streets of Melbourne, a one-eyed fencing contractor in a sea of more qualified unemployed.

After one final and failed attempt at reconciliation with his daughter in which crockery was hurled and a knife pulled on him by her flatmate, Michael left again for the country, saying better a bad life with fresh air than a bad life without. But when he arrived back in the country town of his birth the house he'd left behind had been broken into and vandalised, the furniture smashed, the drawers and cupboards rifled and everything of value gone. He slept on a mattress on the floor with black plastic over the broken windows while he traipsed the surrounding countryside again looking for fencing work or anything else he could find—but again without success. Then one day, returning to his ramshackle house after another fruitless day's searching, he found a man in a suit and tie waiting on his doorstep. They wanted to widen the highway, he said, and were prepared to make an offer. Michael accepted it without hesitation, returned to the city with the money and had already spent the greater part of it on drink, when, as he described it, while standing drunk under a railway bridge one night he saw the dead-end that his life had become and resolved in that moment to do something about it. He bought the paper the following morning, saw the advertisement for the new estate that was about to be opened on the paddocks to the north and, hoping against hope that the farms surrounding this new estate might provide him with the work that those surrounding his home town had so consistently denied him, he packed his bags and put a small deposit down on a house on the corner of South Street and the square.

The freeway meant nothing to Michael, nor the petrol station; he felt no (nor did he want to feel any) connection to the city—in this he was perhaps the only original resident of the estate for whom the catalogue of unkept promises meant nothing. But there the exceptions ended, for like all of us the hoped-for employment continued to elude him. There were three fencing contractors operating from the town up north alone, and they had the business sewn up. It didn't take long for Michael to realise that whatever good may come from his move to the estate it wouldn't come through pursuing his former trade. He gave up trying, lived off his monthly subsidy and the rabbits he shot and, like the rest of us, found whatever distraction he could to fill up the meandering days.

He agreed to build the fence, and I worked alongside him through the remaining weeks of summer. We didn't use the materials in his garage and I never asked him what they were for, but even after a long day's work out on the paddock I would still hear the sawing and hammering drifting from the half-open door as I took my evening stroll. The fence turned out well, though a little crooked. The rabbits would occasionally try to burrow under it but Vito had only to check the perimeter first thing in the morning and drop kerosene and a lit match down any hole he found to forestall any attempt at a break-in. But more important than that was the fact that Michael, who had to some extent always lived on the margins of our community, was now officially inducted into it. He still kept his distance and often sat alone at his own table at Slug's, but the aura of mystery around him gradually dissolved and it was possible to talk to him as, if not a friend, then at least a fellow traveller in the same rudderless boat. One night Nanna even asked him about his family—if he had any, where they were. He had a daughter, he said, but hadn't seen her for some time. Then his eyes grew misty, he fell silent again, and the subject was left alone.

⸻

Though we'd always had trouble with the vandals, that summer the problem grew worse. From your bed at night you might hear the sound of a car engine way out on the access road and the far-off sound of barking dogs. They skirted around the southern edge to the empty houses in West Street and after breaking in would drink their drinks and paint a few slogans on the walls. Sometimes they went further, throwing bricks and shrubs onto the footpaths and driving their cars in screeching circles around one of the empty courts, but we never really felt threatened and accepted it all as a natural consequence of living in such a relatively large, isolated and unguarded place. But late that summer—I think I'm talking about eight years after the opening of the estate here—their nightly invasions suddenly turned nasty.

In one savage night they destroyed the phone box (every window was smashed, the receiver gone) and threw a brick through the window of Slug's. We gathered in the square that morning with a strange disquiet. Of course we were all upset, but Craig seemed to have taken it especially hard—he was crouched beside the phone box with his head held in his hands, a picture of abject despair. I walked over to him and asked him what was wrong. He looked up at me, clearly wondering whether I was the one to whom he should confide his secret. Then he blurted it out.

The phone calls to Paris, which had started out as little more than a drunken harvest-time joke, had become unexpectedly serious. One night his random dialling had put him through to a girl—Marie-Claire, he said, and with such lovelorn sincerity that I didn't know whether to laugh or cry—and as stupid as it may have sounded he had fallen head over heels in love with her. He'd been ringing her every night; she was smitten too; they wanted to get married. He'd asked her to come and live here and it would only have taken a few more calls to arrange it—now his dream was shattered. I tried my best to comfort him—He could always write, I said. But he didn't know her address. Well, just take the car into town, I said, and use the phone box there; you can take the money out of the account. By this time everyone else had gathered around us, their faces a mixture of confusion and concern. What's wrong, said Nanna, has the car been stolen too? I left Craig alone, drew the crowd aside and explained the situation. They all nodded their heads gravely: no question, let him ring from the phone box in town; if he needs to talk to her he can. I went back to tell Craig that the matter was settled and a great weight lifted from him. He drove into town that night with a pocket full of coins and a farewell party wishing him good luck from the gate.

The phone box was irreparable and would probably remain so but no-one wanted to see such a night of destruction again; the brick through the window of Slug's was especially disturbing. So from that night on a new ritual was born. Every evening as the sun went down Michael would bring his rifle to the square and stand sentry there. I found it all a bit melodramatic myself and I tried to talk him in—but he wouldn't listen to me. They're Craig's old friends, he said, don't you see? That's what's upset him most. I won't let it happen again. But do we really need *this*? I asked, pointing too obviously at the rifle. Michael didn't answer, and clutched it a little closer to his chest. Soon I stopped trying to talk sense into him, he would not listen anyway, and I, along with the others, came to accept the sight of him standing out there as part of our daily lives and his ritual pacing of the square at night as one of the many strangenesses with which those lives were now circumscribed. If the vandals from the town up north wanted to try their luck again in the square they would do so at their peril. They didn't: we occasionally heard strange sounds at night from the empty houses in West Court, but otherwise, and for some time yet, they left us conspicuously alone.

five

Though the summer evenings in *ur* were a special time the long cold winters were hard. Icy winds and driving rain blew in across the paddocks, the creek burst its banks and flooded my backyard. Nights at Slug's were almost miserable affairs, Michael outside in his winter coat, the others crammed into the tiny former office with an old towel stuffed into the crack under the door. Dave's frosty beer was undrinkable and most of us turned instead to the gut-warming cheap brandy that now came back from town by the dozen. I spent most days and nights at the kitchen table with my writing: *The Voice* came out sporadically now, enough to give it the status of rare. If Slug's was still open when my work was done I would wander down there for one last drink. Nanna had long since gone to bed with her arthritis wrapped in scarves, Slug was snoring fitfully on the couch he'd installed in the corner for the purpose; Michael's shift was over and he, Craig and Vito were playing their last hand of cards, the biggest pile of matches stacked on the table in front of Craig, while Dave stood idly looking on with a tea towel slung over his shoulder. And it was such a night, a night like that, in the sixth winter since Inauguration and the second since the sewage was diverted, when without warning and to the astonishment of all, Jodie, Michael's daughter, walked into our lives. A sudden blast of cold air accompanied her through the door; all heads turned but no-one spoke. She and Michael stared long and hard at each other before Michael rose from his chair and walked outside with her into the dark.

For three nights following, the arguments rang out, a relentless shouting match that echoed through the deserted streets and sent the dogs into paroxysms of barking. By the fourth night they had exhausted themselves and silence finally reigned in the house. On the morning of the sixth day, with all the bad blood let, Jodie took control of Michael's life and put his house in order. She was a beautiful young woman, her father's daughter, with the same distracted expression and a small fire always smouldering in her case behind both eyes. She gathered up pieces of furniture from the abandoned houses (Michael had almost nothing in his house but an old mattress on the floor) and stocked the kitchen cupboards with food. For the first time since the opening of the estate Nanna found herself a customer: Michael's house was never again seen without flowers in every room. And should you be up early enough in the morning (and in winter few of us were) you would see Michael and Jodie crawling through a hole in a back fence of West Court, crossing the gully of the creek by the footbridge he had laid the previous year, and walking out together across the dew-laden paddocks. They sat together of an afternoon at Slug's and every evening the smell of rabbit stew drifted from their kitchen across the square.

It was enough to restore even the most confirmed cynic's faith in the strange and sometimes troubled world of familial relations—what any of us would have given for a moment of that: with a daughter, son, mother, father, husband or wife. We'd left them all behind: uncles, aunts, cousins too; we had each other, and it was a family of sorts, but the sight of Michael and Jodie often cruelly reminded us that any family, no matter how bonded, interdependent and happy, is an ersatz family compared to the one linked by blood.

In every way Jodie became the new force in our lives, and that winter of her arrival—a sickeningly cold and depressing one—was transformed into a kind of spring. Where normally we would have hibernated for the two months that remained and not felt warm blood in our veins again until Vito organised the first new planting, we suddenly found ourselves in the midst of a flurry of activity. Slug's was repainted and the outside awning extended; six trees—saplings dug up from disused gardens—were planted in the grass block in the centre of the square; the holes in the few streets we still used were re-tarred and the cracks in the gutters and footpaths patched. Michael built a barbed-wire gate to be put up on each of the four streets entering the square to keep the dogs out and a good few were culled as well. (I couldn't tell you how many dogs there were in *ur* at that time; from the few strays that had been left behind when the early residents departed they had bred, inbred and rebred so many times that even the number of cross-breeds was uncountable, let alone the individuals themselves—they had long since killed or chased away all the cats and now roamed the streets in packs, feeding on anything they could find, and with their barking, whining and snapping they often made our lives a misery.) It was not that Jodie was in any way the supervisor or even the instigator of these projects (indeed, the barbed-wire gates were my idea) but by the simple fact of her arrival a new spirit of enterprise had entered into us. All in all, by the time the true spring arrived, we were riding a cresting wave of optimism; the future was before us, a mismanaged past behind. And I, poor fool, had fallen hopelessly in love with Michael's daughter.

Perhaps it was simply an acknowledgement of a deep sense of loneliness long suppressed but my infatuation soon became impossible. (It's an unguarded stairway, easily descended, from the warm house of solitude to the dungeon of loneliness and I had without knowing begun to descend it: I simply spent too much time in the house on North Court on my own.) After a good deal of agonising I finally summoned up the courage to invite her to dinner. It was a week of unseasonal and sporadic rains. She accepted; I took the car keys from Vito and drove into town for the first time in over a year to buy something special for the meal. I had no idea what Michael would make of this, I secretly hoped she wouldn't tell him—to suddenly see him as some kind of father figure was odd in the extreme. I spent all day inside preparing the dinner and deliberately avoiding Slug's. Soft rain was falling when I heard the dogs barking at the North Street gate. Her hair was wet and fell in strands across her shoulders; I offered her a towel which like all my towels gave off a slight swampy smell. We sat opposite each other at the kitchen table, her thin nose casting a curious shadow across one cheek.

After the meal I dispensed with preliminaries and asked her straight out why she had come to *ur* and she answered that she had come to be with her father, to care for him, and to ensure he didn't get into any more trouble. Has he been in trouble before? I asked. But Jodie remained silent. This thing he's building, in his garage. What is it? Jodie just smiled. It's his little joke, that's all, she said. I uncapped a bottle of cheap brandy. Jodie sipped hers and spoke. It's been a running joke in the family, she said, on the male side, for generations. It started with my father's great-grandfather. You know the expression: to be up shit creek in a barbed-wire canoe without a paddle. My great-grandfather fought in the Boer War, when barbed wire was invented by the British to imprison the captured Afrikaners, and came home with his mind in a mess. Apparently, just before he died, he tried to build one of these canoes and sail it up the creek at the back of his property. He nearly drowned, and spent his last weeks in hospital raving like a madman, asking the nurses every morning to fetch his canoe for him: he had an important journey to make. It was all put down to senility, of course, but the thing was that when he died a bundle of papers was found among his things. He'd been making sketches of this canoe for years, the way to launch it, the way to steer it without a paddle, the prayers you were supposed to recite on your way upstream. The papers went to his son and his son after that. And each, apparently, in their final years were struck with the same obsession. On their deathbeds they all asked for this canoe to be brought to them and all died with the same request on their lips. It's been a joke, as I say, to the rest of the family, but it's a joke that won't go away. Dad says he has the old bundle of papers, and he's begun to build the canoe. Is he dying? I asked: does he think he's about to die? Jodie shrugged. She skolled her glass, placed it on the table and walked to the kitchen window. What's that smell? she said.

I'd hoped she wouldn't notice. It was the creek. The vandals had visited earlier in the week and completely destroyed the dam wall that Vito had built to divert the sewage onto his farm. I hadn't told anyone, I was intending to fix it myself. But then I asked Jodie to dinner, everything went a little haywire in my mind, and I kept putting the repairs off; the last thing I was expecting was the sort of rain we'd had over the past couple of days. The creek was up, and even the morning before had been lapping at the back fence.

It's the creek, I said, we've had sewage problems. Jodie continued to stare out the kitchen window into the dark. What are you all doing here? she said after a pause: you could have all left years ago, I don't understand...

Neither do I, I said, but who's to say that things won't change, that a new beginning isn't just around the corner? There was going to be a park over the back fence there, that's why I bought this house in the first place. People ask me why I stay, why I haven't moved down to the square at least; well, it's because I have no real reason to doubt that the park will come one day and I don't see why I shouldn't be here to enjoy it when it does. They say the same thing about the freeway, she said. Yes, I said, and it will come. Jodie looked at me: You still believe in that too? I have to, I said, I couldn't live here otherwise. Everything is possibility; that's what defines this place. Your father too, like all of us, he was hoping to make a new start, and perhaps put that inherited pessimism you spoke of behind him in the process. He's waited this long, and not without reason: you—you are *his* freeway—you have arrived and the wait was worthwhile. It can be the same for all of us, if we show a little patience.

Jodie turned away from the window and I saw the look of the doubter in her eye. It didn't surprise me: how could I hope to prevail upon her when I couldn't even convince myself? She left shortly after and I escorted her to the square. It was a brief goodbye and we didn't touch. I walked back home and drank the last of the brandy alone at the kitchen table with the rain falling softly on the roof.

A barbed-wire canoe? I've never heard anything so ridiculous in my life. He's just building a fence, that's all, to keep his hand in. Jodie's imagination was even more fertile than mine, and suddenly my love for her increased tenfold accordingly. Who could not love someone who had the mind to invent a story like that?

Eventually I washed the dishes—amazed at having two each of everything—and allowed myself the occasional wistful smile as I gazed out the kitchen window into the dark. Around eleven I put on my raincoat and gumboots, took a shovel from the shed, jumped the back fence and walked briskly through the mud to the dam.

six

It was summer again, Vito was out on the paddock picking beans when he saw the cloud of dust off in the east, somewhere near the highway. He watched it for four days, moving imperceptibly closer before he asked me to come out one afternoon and look. It rose as a whitish cloud and drifted slowly south on the breeze. We walked together down the access road and in the distance we could hear the diesel engines revving. Two bulldozers and a grader: they were carving a road from the highway across the paddocks towards *ur*.

I was convinced it was just a driveway to a new farmhouse about to be built in off the highway. It was not the best land in the district but that didn't stop someone from setting up house there. The paddocks around *ur* contained a smattering of livestock and we often heard and sometimes saw a motorbike driving a herd of cows or half a dozen horses from one paddock to another. So there was no reason why one of the owners of these paddocks (whom we'd always imagined living somewhere further north) shouldn't want to build a house on his land, perhaps the easier to get working on the soil which had been neglected for so long. Vito kept me posted; each day the machinery crept closer. There was no hiding it from the others any more and they came out each day to the access road to look. The work seemed to stop for a day, just short of Vito's garden, then the following morning they began excavating a large area—about the size of a small football field and three to four metres deep—at the end of the road they'd already dug. Late that afternoon the machinery left and the only malevolent consequences for us seemed to be the cloud of dust that was lifted late each afternoon by the breeze and drifted in over our houses. Then one morning about two weeks later we awoke to the sound of a truck engine and a strange putrid smell. I was the first out on the access road: the truck was disappearing behind a cloud of dust and in the hole was an enormous pile of household rubbish.

Each day the truck arrived and dumped another load of rubbish in the hole. Within a week the flies were hanging above it in a thick black moving cloud. A meeting was called but no-one knew what to say: someone was turning the outskirts of *ur* into a tip and we seemed powerless to stop it. The paddocks surrounding *ur* had always been government-owned and had been bought along with the original estate site in anticipation of further expansion, but when it was obvious that this expansion wouldn't come—when all eyes turned to the east—the land had been leased back to a couple of local farmers who used it for grazing their stock. Now, it seemed, the local shire had bought this land from the government and set aside a portion to use, yes, as a tip.

The next day I wrote and posted a letter to the government department that I believed responsible for the fiasco, threatening further action unless pressure was brought to bear on the shire to cease this unsanitary practice. I have no idea what communications then flew back and forth between government and shire—they flew, as it were, above our heads—but shortly after, a four-page reply from the government department in question was delivered to *ur* (they didn't know who to deliver it *to* and slipped it quietly under the door of Slug's). It said, in effect, that a regrettable mistake had been made in selling the land to the shire, that it was certainly done without knowledge of the manner in which it would be used, that the land had now been repurchased, the person responsible sacked, and that we may rest assured that the area surrounding the *Outer Suburban Village Development Complex*, including the large tract of land southward originally purchased for use as a freeway, will be retained by the department until such time as it can be put to its intended use. The letter was handed around at Slug's that night and we all breathed a collective sigh of relief.

But our relief was premature; a week later the rubbish truck arrived again and the dumping continued daily. We confronted the garbage men out on the paddock but they just shrugged their shoulders and drove away. Soon a tip attendant was set up permanently on the site with his makeshift hut and bulldozer. We could get nothing out of him either but a well-meaning apology: he was just doing his job, he said, it was out of his hands, he didn't know any more than us why they'd decided to put the tip here. After more than a dozen unanswered letters to the government asking for action to be taken against the shire and to the shire threatening government action—I myself became exhausted by the whole thing and left it to find its own resolution. The rest of *ur* showed little more enthusiasm for this sudden brush with bureaucracy; we'd lived so long now without such nonsense that everyone found it difficult to readjust. There was a rubbish tip next door; it was extraordinary when I think back on it just how easily we adapted to this fact. By a kind of osmosis the tip had become part of our lives; we soon forgot how, why, or even when, and accepted the fact as given.

It was a good indication of the collective state of mind in *ur* at the time. I myself had become more and more detached from this strange half-begun, half-finished housing estate that had originally promised so much. We had tried to adapt, were still trying to adapt, but the fact remained that no amount of adaptation could ever compensate for the fact that the basic idea was wrong. We were living *wrongly*, pretending it was right, and the greatest tragedy of all was that we could not see it. I'd fallen in love with Jodie, had had her over for dinner, but under these impossible circumstances could I ever really hope to win her? It was not a subsiding house on the edge of a creek in a housing estate fifty kilometres north of Melbourne that I needed to achieve this up-to-now elusive goal, but a house in a verdant suburb in the east, with the bees buzzing above the flowerbeds and a sprinkler turning lazily on the lawn. *Then* she might take me seriously and forget about her father and his peculiar miseries, stop filling her head with stories that pretended to explain them.

Yes, I was thinking of leaving, the first time that such a thought had seriously entered my head. I hardly ventured down to the square any more for my usual drink at Slug's,

I stayed home most nights and did little else but plan my next meal with Jodie and the proposal I would put to her over dessert. But I could not get the tip off my mind. And so, one hot, muggy summer's night, unable to sleep, I put on my clothes, found my torch and went walking down the access road. I would normally have walked the ring road on such a night—its circularity seemed to calm me: after two or three times round I'd finally find myself breathing easier and the door to sleep would open. But that night all my thoughts were of the tip and I felt inexorably drawn towards it. As I passed it on my left I saw a light outside the hut and a figure—the tip attendant, Alex—sitting by the door. He raised his hand and waved to me; I raised my torch and waved back. He shouted: Come over for a drink! I hesitated for a moment, then picked my way across the empty paddocks and shook his filthy hand. Well, he said, sit down—and pointed to a rickety old wooden chair. A cut-down forty-four-gallon drum, half-filled with cold ash and charred lumps of wood, was propped up on bricks between us. He'd somehow laid his hands on some beer from Slug's, by what route I couldn't say. He emerged from the hut with a fresh glass and poured me one. Cheers, he said, and as I raised my glass the crack from top to bottom caught the light of the hurricane lamp. I don't like going down into the square, he said, so it's nice to have a visitor drop by. The smell of rotting garbage hung in the warm still air.

What do you think of us? I asked after a silence: to you people in town this must all look a bit strange. Strange, he said, what do you mean strange? I mean strange to an outsider like you. I'm not so much of an outsider, said Alex. Not now perhaps, I said, but before. Not before either, he said. I don't follow you, I said. I'm Jean's son, he said. Who's Jean? Nanna, said Alex, my mother. You've been Nanna's son all along? All along, said Alex with a smile, ever since I was born; I encouraged her to buy her house here in the first place—didn't you know that every time Craig goes into town he takes a letter from Mum to me and one from me back to Mum with her allowance? Her allowance? I said. I give her half my wage every week, said Alex. (Well, what on earth does she do with it? I thought.) I've known Craig for a long time, Alex continued, he used to sleep in a car at the old tip, near the cemetery in town; I suggested he grab one of the empty houses on the estate—they were there for the taking, after all. Poor boy, he's in love, isn't he? With a girl from Paris! He tells me he's been studying French; she's already saved half the airfare and should be out here soon. Good luck to him—he's the only one that might get what he wants out of all of this in the end.

So he was here in the early days? And yes, suddenly I did remember him, vaguely, accompanying Nanna, helping her with the shop, but he was younger then, and cleaner: altogether different. He must have left some time in the second year and found a job at the tip up north. Like so many, I thought, wondering then how many others like Alex still retained some connection. Are there still dozens out there, on the farms, in the small one-shop towns, biding their time, waiting to come home? It seemed extraordinary that Alex himself could have kept up contact with his mother all that time and then by such a roundabout route end up moving back to *ur*. Or almost. For despite the fact that Nanna still lived in a large and otherwise empty three-bedroom house just a stone's throw away, Alex persisted in sleeping in his hut. On the outside walls he'd hung bits and pieces of junk he'd scavenged from the tip—old kettles, children's toys, steam irons, dish drainers, saucepans with pink geraniums cascading from them, bicycle wheels, hub caps—and on the roof a crop of wandering jew spread and hung from a sump filled with soil. The path to the front door was lined with the cut-off humps of car tyres painted white; to the door itself he'd fitted a frying pan knocker, and above the doorway a mobile made from fishing line and tappets tinkled in the breeze.

So Craig has always known, I said, about you, I mean? Yes, he said, I'd regularly fix him up with parts for the car—you think he could have kept Vito's old station wagon going for you otherwise?—and he'd bring me a few bottles of Dave's home brew. There's more to this relocation of the tip than I've been able to figure out yet, I said, still not sure where I was taking the conversation. It had nothing to do with me, Bram, said Alex, you know that; I just work for them. What the shire does, in cahoots with the government or not, has nothing to do with me. So you think the government is behind it? I said. Maybe, I don't know, said Alex: they'll have to find some way of shifting you all eventually and getting rid of this blot on the landscape.

It was strange, but they were the words I'd been waiting for, the words I'd wanted to hear. Because deep in my heart I believed them: *ur* had become a grotesquerie, and the most grotesque part about it was that we who lived there couldn't see it. A blot on the landscape, is that what you think we've become, I said, and the government and the shire are trying to remove all traces of us with a tip...? Did I say that? said Alex: I didn't say that, it's just an expression, that's all. But you're right, I said, I believe it too. Have you got any idea what the new eastern suburbs must look like by now, compared to this?—and with a sweep of my hand I gestured towards the collection of houses behind us, strange and spectral in the moonlight. It breaks my heart to think about it. Look at it: a barren, childless place—it's five years now since the last kid left. We've got no school, no playground, no park; ride your bike in the street and you'd be eaten by the dogs. There can never be children here, and without children, a new generation in which to pour all our hopes and dreams, the rot in *ur*'s heart will eat it away. We've become grotesque. Look at your mother: I don't mean to sound cruel but anywhere else, a shopping mall in the east, a stall at a school fête, it would be the most natural and most beautiful thing in the world—an old lady selling flowers—but here it's monstrous, absurd. She's barely sold twenty bunches since the estate began; they sit in her buckets till the petals go brown then end up on the compost heap with all the rest. Look at this, here, now: I'm talking to you, a tip attendant, with a stinking pile of rubbish outside, barely two hundred metres from my house, which with the sewage outfall at the best of times stinks like an open sewer. And has anyone done anything about it aside from using the sludge to grow vegetables, which—I don't know if you've noticed—are now going to seed in the paddock behind us, unpicked...?

Alex was nodding off, a day's work done and three bottles of beer under his belt; he tried to open his eyes to me but they just rolled back in his head and the lids fell slowly over them. I slept there that night, with a blanket on the floor, and only woke late the following morning at the sound of the rubbish truck dumping its load. Alex was up and I stood in the doorway and watched him talking to the driver in the cabin, his foot propped up on the step, a cigarette hanging from his lip. There was the foul taste of a hangover in my mouth and my clothes gave off a faint whiff of kerosene. The smell of the newly dumped load of rubbish made me turn away to retch.

That morning, for the first time in years, I felt the will to go on drain completely from me. My knees seemed to buckle. I sat on the chair outside Alex's door and watched, as if dreaming, while the truck drove away and Alex climbed up into the seat of the bulldozer and started it up with a splutter and a puff of black smoke. I called out to him—I'm off now!—but he had a pair of earmuffs clamped to his head. He turned the dozer around and began spreading the pile of rubbish.

As I cut across the paddocks towards home I saw Vito in the garden, making his way along a row of yellowing Brussels sprouts. I waved to him, and he to me. By the time I reached my front door I was retching uncontrollably again.

seven

Two weeks later the vandals arrived. Michael was in bed. They started up Alex's bulldozer in the middle of the night, drove it down the access road and through the eastern gate straight into the front wall of Slug's, where they helped themselves to the spirits from the shelves and a small amount of cash from the drawer. Dave was already sweeping up the splinters of glass from the footpath when Alex came down to retrieve his machine. I pulled him aside and confronted him straight out: Did he or did he not lend the vandals the bulldozer so that they could wreak this havoc? No, said Alex, a little desperately, and he leaned down under the dash and pulled out two stray wires. Look, he said. He touched the wires together and the motor burst into life, forcing the others who had gathered around to jump back in fright. Any young yahoo would know how to do it, Alex shouted above the sound of the engine: do you expect me to sleep in the cabin with a loaded shotgun? Turn it off, I said. Alex did, and the motor idled, coughed, spluttered and died. They've broken the gearstick, he said, almost sadly, and wobbled it with his hand: they probably didn't mean to end up here but just lost control and bailed out. They've stolen every bottle we had, Slug chimed in, indignantly, and the takings from the drawer—I think they knew what they were doing. A solemn nodding of heads confirmed it.

The following day I arranged to meet Michael in an empty house in West Court, well away from the occupied houses and the square. It felt unusually clandestine and was probably unnecessary anyway; the others were busy for most of the day cleaning up the mess at Slug's. Michael was already waiting for me when I arrived, sitting on the front porch of a house that—like all the others in West Court—had had every window broken, the front door torn from its hinges, and bottles and cans strewn among the waist-high weeds in the garden. We walked inside and sat on the empty lounge-room floor. Flies buzzed in zigzag patterns around the broken light fitting; the smell of stale urine was almost unbearable. I've spoken to Alex, Michael, I said, and if I can read between the lines I'm sure he thinks that the rubbish tip is a calculated move to get rid of us. Something has got to be done. Michael nodded, with apparent understanding. It all makes perfect sense, I said, we've become an embarrassment, they can't let us go on. These vandals are not vandals at all—I'm convinced of this now—they are being paid by the shire or the government or both to make our life here untenable and eventually force us out. Michael stared at me for a moment, then turned and looked out the window. And why are you telling me all this, he said: is it because you are in love with my daughter? I blushed, and tried to regain my composure. Michael gave me a devilish grin. Leave it with me, he said.

Shortly after, as the first of the autumn rains began sweeping in across the paddocks, Michael started building the wall. I had neither the presence of mind nor the wherewithal to stop him. He seconded Alex and his bulldozer (at the point of a gun, as I later discovered) and had him knock down half a dozen empty houses on the edge of South-East Court. He sorted the good bricks from the rubble, ferried mud for mortar from the creek, and day by day the wall grew higher. It rose on the outer edge of the ring road, with the footpath for a foundation, and one by one over the winter that followed all the houses outside its confines were demolished to provide the bricks. Michael worked every day until the light gave out, often in the drizzling rain, carting mud from the western branch of the creek on a flat-topped barrow made from scraps of wood and an old bicycle wheel and laying bricks with a home-made trowel. A few of the others tried to talk him in—we feared for his health above all—but Michael could not be swayed. The wall eventually rose to thirty courses, over two metres high, and *ur* was in the end contained exclusively within the confines of the old ring road, its size reduced by more than half. As Alex's bulldozer bore down on the last house left standing in North Court I resigned myself to the inevitable, packed up my things and moved to a vacant house on the corner of North Street and the square, diagonally opposite Slug's. Closer to Jodie, I remember thinking, as if that were any consolation.

As winter drew to a close, Michael topped the wall with a tangle of barbed wire and broken beer bottles and constructed a huge barbed-wire gate to stop up the access road entrance. With the first days of spring Vito began planting his new crop in the square (he'd already dug up all the front lawns of West Street in preparation for his new system of rotation): the last vegetables had been picked from the old farm and it would now be abandoned. *ur* had become, by a roundabout route, the village it had never been before, and now within the confines of Michael's wall its security seemed assured. Some of my forebodings diminished; there was still reason to hope. I cleaned out my new house and unpacked my things. But then, like all the lights flickering in all the houses of a vast suburb before the power fails, there followed a series of otherwise unrelated events that could only be read as premonitory signs of the great upheaval to come.

Slug left, just like that, without so much as a word. Dave opened the bar one morning to find a note stuck to the fridge: for two days the bar remained closed and the eerie sense that something was wrong hung about the square. On the third day, when Dave re-emerged, he was a shadow of his former self. It was Craig who finally extracted the news from him. Slug had gone back to Melbourne and his former wife to revive his real estate business. The note to Dave was like a bill of divorce, concerned mostly, it seemed, with assuring him that the bar would be his and that he, Slug, would make no future claim on either the property or the business. He hoped this would ensure that the parting was an amicable one and wished him all the best for the future. The bar was eventually reopened but not before all trace of Slug's influence had been wiped away—from that day on he became *ur*'s much-needed *bête noir*. The old sign was taken down and a new one—*Dave's*—put up in its place; the padlocks were removed from the fridges and the beer came out again. Dave had aged—Slug's departure had aged him all the more—but his spirit had not been broken. He again threw himself into the daily tasks of brewing, bottling and serving like a man who wants no time to think.

Late one afternoon around this time a herd of cows wandered in off the paddocks through the open gate and stood around dreamily chewing their cud in the square. Like a harbinger, I thought, when I saw them that day. They were quickly chased away by Vito and no great damage was done, but it was an irony not lost on us that this kind of thing had never happened before: it was as if the very presence of the wall had encouraged the incursion. The gate was bolted behind them again but every day they gathered outside, a brave few sometimes lurching forward and pushing themselves against the wire. (There is nothing so disconcerting in my memory as the eyes of those thirty-odd cows staring at us from the other side of the gate as we picked the first new crop in the square that summer; I hope I can one day erase it forever.) Then, early one morning a few days later, the final presentiment. Craig excused himself from that morning's picking with 'business to attend to' and drove the car off down the access road, honking the horn excitedly at Alex as he passed. He came back two hours later from the airport with Marie-Claire. She was a plumpish girl, a good deal younger than Craig (who I think was about thirty at the time) and spoke barely a word of English. Don't worry, Craig said, as we gathered in the square, she already felt perfectly at home. She'd seen the sign out on the access road: *ur*. Her parents, he explained, had come from a village of the same name in the Pyrenees, near the border with Spain; she felt as if, by the long way round, she'd returned to her childhood home. Though still a little dumbfounded (surely it was time to go, not come), that evening we all gathered at Dave's to celebrate her arrival. Vito produced a bottle of red wine that, as he said, had been gathering dust under his house for the past decade, and ceremoniously uncorked it; he raised a toast in Italian, Marie-Claire responded in French, and through the long and drunken night that followed Craig acted as tireless interpreter in the strangest series of conversations the old bar had ever witnessed. I stood a little outside all this, slumped in the corner, a dispassionate observer. Why had I stayed? Through the long cold winter of the wall, the lonely nights in the new North Street house, without producing a single copy of *The Voice*? Aside from Jodie and the hopes I had for us, what was there left for me here? I watched the frivolity surrounding Marie-Claire's arrival as one who is already drifting away.

⸻

Two days later Craig, Marie-Claire and I drove into town: she wanted to call her parents to tell them she'd arrived safely; I had business at the bank. I was withdrawing the money from the *ur* account—the accumulated monthly subsidies that the government had been paying us—and closing it for good. This, I believed, and the conversation I would have with Jodie when I returned, were all that now stood between this intolerable present and the new future I had planned. I left Craig and Marie-Claire at the phone box and walked up the main street to the bank—but when I got to the window they told me that no such account existed. I argued with them—It must exist, I said, I opened it myself—but they held their ground. I turned and walked out empty-handed into the street. Craig and Marie-Claire were still in the phone box, Marie-Claire stooped forward with the receiver to one ear and her hand pressed tightly against the other. I stood at the car and leaned on the bonnet. Now? I heard myself saying: go now? Craig held one finger up and pointed at his watch. I slipped into the front seat and waited.

When we arrived back in *ur* all was chaos. Vito greeted us at the gate with panic in his eyes. We've had a visitor, he said, Michael's holding him at his house.

We drove through the open gate to Michael's house on South Street where Jodie, Dave and Nanna were gathered outside on the lawn. There was almost a party atmosphere: Dave had brought a table and some chairs from the café and empty bottles lay scattered on the grass. Had we been in town that long? The small crowd fell silent as I strode towards the front door, conscious above all of Jodie's eyes upon me and of assuming an authoritative air. The flyscreen door banged shut behind me.

In the lounge room a stranger was sitting in an armchair with one leg propped up on the coffee table. Opposite him, in another armchair, sat Michael. The blinds were partly drawn and, though it was already a stinking summer's afternoon outside, the room was dark and cool. I nodded to Michael and looked at the stranger, whose brow was wet with perspiration: he kept lifting a handkerchief to his face and wiping it away. The man was forty-odd, with slightly receding hair. He was dressed in a suit and tie—though the collar had been loosened—and I could see a black briefcase on the floor beside him. I was waiting for you to get back before we went any further, said Michael: pull up a chair. I brought a chair from the kitchen where Dave peered in through the window at me with a questioning look. I gestured to him as if to say: Be patient, we'll just have to wait and see. When I returned to the lounge room, with my eyes now better accustomed to the dark inside the house, I noticed for the first time why the stranger's leg was propped up on the coffee table. His sock and shoe were gone, the trouser leg was rolled up to the knee and a packet of frozen peas was moulded onto the ankle. The bruise was already coming out. Michael caught my eye and by way of explanation said: He tripped. I drew up my chair. This is Layland, said Michael: he's on an errand from the city. Layland, Bram, our resident intellectual. The tone of voice was so sinister—I'd never heard anything like it from Michael before—that Layland could only manage a half-smile in response before raising the handkerchief to his brow again. Layland says we should have received a letter, Bram, said Michael: do you know anything about that? A letter? No, I said, where's a letter going to come from, the sky? We haven't seen a postman here in over a decade. Layland was not amused. I don't know anything about that, he said, if the letter hasn't arrived that's not my fault. It should have, that's all. It was sent, I saw it sent myself. But the point is—as I've tried to explain to Michael here—that I was sent here to go over the details of this letter and help you in any way I can. Now, if the letter hasn't arrived, all right, there's really no point in my being here, is there? I will go back to the office, tell them the letter hasn't arrived and if necessary come back in a week's time when it has. It's no skin off my nose. I'm only here to help. So he's serious, I thought, they have sent a letter—but what postman in his right mind would have braved the wall and the barbed-wire gate to deliver it? Quite honestly, I said, I don't see the point in waiting for a letter that will probably never arrive anyway. And if you've come to explain the details of this letter then you must know its contents. I can't see why you can't just give us the news yourself. He already has, Michael interrupted. I already have, Layland echoed, against my better judgment and, I might add, under duress. I looked at Michael; he looked away. And on a point of principle, continued Layland, I'm not going to repeat it. It was completely outside my brief to break the news to you in the first place—I was sent here to go over the details, that's all. He was raising his voice now, and perspiring badly. Michael softly grabbed my arm and ushered me out into the hallway; Layland slumped back into the armchair, looked at his ankle and winced.

Michael drew me into the kitchen. The sound of Layland's voice had brought Dave to the window again. Michael pointed at his watch as if to say: It won't be long—and Dave disappeared again. Michael leaned against the kitchen bench. Well, Bram, he said, the story is this. They want to demolish *ur*. They're planning another

Estate, bigger and better they say, fifty kilometres north-west of us. The freeway, they say, is finally coming. But here's the joke: it's going to pass straight through us, six lanes wide, and link up with this new estate—a satellite town they're calling it. We're being offered homes and the old petrol subsidies again if we want to move there, but the fact is, whether we take up this offer or not, *ur* is going to be destroyed. You were right about the tip, the shire was trying to get rid of us. They'd been putting pressure on the government for years but when the tip didn't move us, well, they turned the screws a little harder and now it looks like the government has finally buckled. I think it's all a trick, of course. There'll be no freeway, no satellite town, we'll all be 'temporarily housed' while *ur* is demolished and then we'll all be forgotten again. But I'm not trying to influence you one way or the other. I've already told everyone outside what's going on and we all have to make up our own minds about it. I'm sure you know where I stand. And just to get something clear: he knocked on my door first, you were in town. I said we'd never seen any such letter and then got the news out of him anyway. I asked him to wait while the others were told—in case they had any questions. He was getting all uptight and wanted to go. I told him he had to wait for you and Craig to get back from town. He made a run for it and fell off the front porch, there was nothing more to it than that. I've told him he can stay here the night and, if he likes, someone can drive him back tomorrow. You talk to him if you want, and make up your own mind. I'm sure the others have told Craig by now, I'll go out and see how he's taking it.

I went back into the lounge room and took a chair opposite Layland. You must understand Mr...he said. Bram, I said. You must understand, Bram, Layland began, that I've only been sent here to go over the details. This has been a very trying time for me—and he reached down and touched his ankle as if to indicate what he meant. He seemed to have relaxed a little, he'd taken off his suit jacket and put his handkerchief away but the ankle was obviously still giving him trouble: he shifted his leg and readjusted the makeshift icepack, now soggy and unfrozen. I could hear the low murmur of voices outside. Layland, apparently conscious of them, was speaking almost in a whisper. But now that it's fallen to me to break the news myself, he said, I think I should make a few points very clear. You seem like a sensible person, Bram—he glanced towards the window where the curtains were still drawn as if to draw some not-too-subtle comparison between myself and the others—and I don't think my words will be wasted. The fact is, this has to be seen as a very favourable turn of events for you all. I can tell you now, honestly, that the government has felt very bad about the planning mistakes that were made here in the first place and has been searching for years now for a way to correct them and in some way compensate you all for the distress these mistakes have caused. What you have here is an extremely generous offer. I've seen the plans for this satellite town and, I'm not just saying this, I've already discussed it with my wife—I will be the first person standing in line for a house there, you can rest assured on that. This place here was an experiment, granted, and I think you would also grant that it has been a terrible failure. But what use is an experiment if we can't learn from it? The new development has been thoroughly thought out, thanks in the main to a close and careful study of the mistakes made here and a determination not to have them repeated. You will own your own home, petrol subsidies will be provided, there will be business and employment opportunities aplenty. I've seen the plans, I assure you. And, well, to be perfectly frank, I'm a little surprised at the reception I've got here. You would think I was the bearer of bad news rather than good. It surprises me, I have to say...Just then, as if on cue, the screen door slammed and Dave entered with a bottle of beer and two frosty glasses on a tray. He placed it on the coffee table beside Layland's foot and quietly left again. I poured a glass each. Well, yes, Bram, continued Layland, all I can say is that if you have any influence here at all, and I suspect you might, I would urge you to use this influence on the others. This is a very generous offer. Of course, as you know, your homes here will be demolished. But it makes perfect sense, I'm sure you'll agree, that the tract of land already purchased for the original freeway should be used, and that by bringing it through here and then diverting it slightly north-west along the new fifty-kilometre tract of land we are in the process of purchasing we can deliver it to the new satellite town at very little additional cost. But I don't need to explain all that to you, I'm sure. The fact is that the old estate here will have to go anyway, and we might as well kill two birds with one stone. And, really, I know this must all be something of a shock to you now but, a year from now, say, will anyone be shedding any tears? Brick walls, barbed-wire gates, vandalised houses, leaking sewage, a rubbish tip on your doorstep; you may feel some attachment to it at the moment but I don't think you'll be feeling too nostalgic about it when it's gone. There's no hurry, of course, we're not asking you to pack up and move overnight but I need hardly remind you that, having learned from our mistakes as I was mentioning before, a firm decision has already been made to build the freeway *first* this time before embarking on the development at the other end, so, well, as you can see, your time is limited to some extent and in the meantime I would urge you to use what influence...

Michael had walked back into the room and Layland suddenly fell silent. It was barely a glance that Michael threw at me but I knew straight away that in his opinion I'd already spent too long with Layland. I turned and walked back out into the sunshine, squinting my eyes against the light. As I stood on the porch, with my neighbours arrayed on the lawn in front of me, it was the sight of Marie-Claire with her head on Craig's shoulder, weeping, that affected me most. All the way from Paris, for this. I went down onto the lawn to share a beer with them all and eat the snacks that Nanna had prepared. The memory of Inauguration Day and the opening gala came back to me: the drinks, the savouries, the fresh hopeful faces, the speeches, and that small crowd, almost replicated here, who stayed on under the marquee as the shadows lengthened to joke and laugh and form the first tentative friendships against the uncertainties to come. And yes, here we were again, this time on Michael's front lawn as the afternoon faded and the last crumbs were picked from the plates. I put my arm around Marie-Claire and gently patted her shoulder. *Très bon*, I said, knowing no other French, and she smiled up at me through her tears. I walked over to Jodie and drew her aside. I was going to leave, I said, and ask you to come with me. But it looks like that plan might have to be shelved. She smiled at me. Why would you want to leave now? she said, not bothering to hide her sarcasm: the freeway is coming; isn't that what you've been waiting for? Maybe the park will be next...She lingered a moment, with a glint in her eye, then turned and went inside.

Layland stayed that night; Jodie made up a bed for him on the lounge-room floor. A few remained drinking out on the lawn well after the sun had set and that night Dave's remained closed for the first time since its former owner's departure. I took my evening stroll around the ring road, checking the wall here and there, stopping to tap at a loose-looking course of bricks or to kick around at the base to see that the foundations were secure. How my evening stroll had changed from those evenings long ago! Around the entire perimeter the wall rose up beside me; no more vistas of paddocks, grazing cows and horses, rabbits hopping among the gorse in the last of the evening light. Thirty courses of house bricks, hastily laid, and beyond a world fading from memory with the fading of the light. I stopped at the gate and peered through the barbed wire. A cow lowed long and far away. In the faint orange glow from the drum outside his hut I could just make out Alex standing, rubbing his hands and then offering them to the fire. As if accepting a gift, he then claimed it by rubbing. The bulldozer looked like some strange enormous animal, jaw open, teeth bared, waiting to strike. What days ahead! What little sense I had of them as I stood at the gate that night.

eight

I have to record, now, that no-one left *ur* and no-one arrived for the next two hundred and twenty-three days. That's how long it went on. It began in the most quiet and subtle way, as I suppose all these things do. Layland's ankle was bad: by the following day it had swelled to almost three times its normal size; there was no question of him moving. The following morning his car was brought in off the access road and parked inside the East Wall. Something had changed in him during the night, I imagine he'd hardly slept and had gone over a good many things in his mind; he now seemed to accept the fact of his confinement with equanimity. He hardly had cause for complaint. Jodie fluffed up his pillows and renewed the icepack, Nanna brought him a tray of freshly baked biscuits and the room was filled with flowers. I visited him that lunchtime and he greeted me with an almost apologetic smile. I asked would he like us to call someone for him, his wife perhaps, Craig could take the car and use the phone box in town. He waved his hand as if waving the very idea out of the room: he was not on good terms with his wife, she'd hardly miss him and if she did, well and good, let her worry, it won't do her any harm at all, perhaps she might see through that cuckold and in his, Layland's, absence begin to understand again what a good and faithful husband he'd been. I pursued the matter no further. I asked him if he was comfortable—to which he replied: Yes, very—and suggested that we leave any further discussion of yesterday's business until he was feeling better. He was welcome to stay, as long as was needed; he would not find us lacking in hospitality. On the outside, I said—I had to allow myself this—we might look like a hard-bitten bunch but you would never find us throwing a guest out on the street. He dismissed the very idea. He'd had plenty of time to think during the night, he said—the ankle had kept him awake—and had changed his mind about many things. He would accept our hospitality, with gratitude. I let him know with a nod of my head that this was undoubtedly the wisest course of action and left him alone to rest.

⁂

Michael was like a man on hot coals and it took all my best efforts to calm him down. He had called a meeting at Dave's that morning and insisted that no-one was leaving until someone superior in Layland's department provided a written guarantee of the compensation he was offering. We've heard enough hot-air promises already, Michael said: either they give it to us in writing or we won't be moving an inch. No-one dared argue with him, indeed, there was, if anything, complete agreement with the stand he was proposing to take (it was hard to believe in any kind of offer any more, let alone one as generous as this) but nor do I think anyone knew at the time where this ultimatum would lead us. Everyone nodded their heads, but on every face I could see a furrowed brow.

Within two weeks Layland was up and walking again, on a pair of crutches improvised by Craig. He sometimes drank with us in the afternoon at Dave's and was in the most discreet way possible including himself gradually in the new village life. His presence was tolerated to a fair extent and I think many of us were grateful in a way to have him there; he seemed to offer us protection of some sort. So long as he remained our guest we could hope no moves would be made against us. But no such excuses for Layland were forthcoming from Michael; he could not stand the sight of the man, so deeply had the news affected him, and through all that time I did not see him once look Layland in the eye. This simmering tension had to come to a head—and sooner than expected, it did. Michael was drunk, that has to be taken into account: he had been drinking at Dave's all afternoon. Layland came in late that evening and asked Dave for two bottles to take home with him, a harmless request in itself. But Michael suddenly exploded. He accused Layland of being a leech, of sucking the blood from the very thing he would have soon destroyed completely. In an instant Layland reverted to the awkward visitor we'd seen sitting in Michael's lounge room with his leg propped up on the coffee table that hot day three weeks before. His cheeks grew flushed, he broke out in a sweat, he gestured vaguely and stammered but no words came from his mouth. Michael went on: what right did he have, an agent of our enemies, to come here and eat our food and drink our beer while back in the office where he was probably no more than a trifling functionary, an unreliable drunkard who had been passed over for promotion a hundred times, back there in that office shut off from the realities of life where they were at this very moment preparing the plans for our destruction, what right did he have, a grovelling worm, to assume the status of guest as if it were his God-given right? Layland stepped back, and stammered again. He paused, then turned on his heels, walked out the door and crossed the square towards his car parked over by the East Wall. Let him go, said Michael, still seated at his table. Some of us walked to the door. Layland reached his car, threw himself into the driver's seat and turned the key: the motor whined but it wouldn't start. The battery's flat, said Craig at my shoulder: it's been sitting too long. Layland got out again, slammed the door behind him and walked towards the gate. I heard the scrape of a chair behind me. Layland fumbled with the lock on the gate but he couldn't open it; he started to scramble up, we heard his trousers tear, then the sound of a shot ringing out. Layland stopped—everything stopped—then, more desperately now, he tried to climb up over the gate again. Down the road at the tip, we heard Alex's bulldozer start up and saw its lights come on. Michael was now striding across the square, a rifle in his hand. Layland flung himself from the top of the gate but as he hit the ground on the other side his weak ankle went on him again and in the lights of the approaching bulldozer we could see him hopping around in a circle, one trouser leg flapping. He looked down the road, caught like a frightened rabbit in the lights, then hobbled off across the wasteland outside the wall where the rubble from the demolished houses of South-East Court still lay. Michael reached the gate, poked the rifle through it, took aim and fired.

It was only a flesh wound, the other leg this time, but Layland was unable to take another step. He was carried back to Michael's house, Craig and Alex forming a fireman's cradle, and laid out on his bed in the lounge room. Marie-Claire quickly cleaned and bandaged the wound, and Jodie renewed the icepack on his ankle, as each of us shuffled softly into the room and stood around the walls. The room was eerily quiet. Michael entered, still carrying his rifle, and Layland visibly stiffened as he crossed to the vacant armchair opposite and sat cradling it in his lap. I was about to speak, still unsure of what I was going to say, when suddenly the room went dark. What's happened? said someone in the darkness. Someone else lit a match: The lights have gone, they've cut the power.

Two hundred and twenty-three days is a long time, by anyone's reckoning, and we thought they'd never end. The world beyond the wall receded even further from us, birds flew high above; we occasionally heard the distant sound of an engine and sometimes even a voice carried like a wisp on the wind, but throughout that time it's the silence inside *ur* I'll always remember most. We stayed in our houses or if we went out at all we did so in our slippers, afraid to break the spell of silence with the clumsy sounds of footfall. The autumn rains came; we watched them fall from our kitchen windows or together, in silence, at Dave's. No-one would be leaving, that much was certain, but under these circumstances and in the depths of our hearts no-one knew any more what it meant to stay.

In the midst of all this silence the most silent of all was Layland. It was as if he'd been struck dumb. He wrote out his requests on slips of paper that he handed to Jodie (he would have nothing to do with Michael, not even via this elliptic form of communication). He lay on the lounge-room floor all day with the blinds drawn, unable to move. Jodie brought him his food, Marie-Claire cleaned his wound and changed the bandage and Layland suffered these daily rituals in silence. He was a terrible sight, and as much as we may have resented him and all he had come to stand for, at the same time we couldn't help feeling some sympathy for his plight. He'd obviously been a great talker in his day, had been sent to *ur* precisely on that account (the great talkers always get the dirtiest jobs), and to see him now wrapped in silence, pale, feeble and a shadow of himself, couldn't fail to move even the stoniest heart to pity. For this reason he was allowed some liberties which might otherwise have seemed unthinkable. His wound and consequent immobility hadn't dulled his appetite and the great majority of his request slips were for food. Against our better judgment we invariably acceded to them. It wasn't easy; had the sight of him not stirred up a kind of collective guilt for what Michael had done we'd gladly have seen him starve. We ourselves were facing this disturbing prospect and it grew more disturbing by the day.

Of course, the plan was clear: they would make our life impossible and eventually starve us out. We had no intention of leaving voluntarily: if they wanted to put their freeway through *us* and build their satellite town they would have to get rid of us first. The plan was a good one, and we were already feeling its effects. The wall might be a protection against the vandals and any other form of violent assault but it could do nothing to stop the slow rot that was now eating us away from the inside. With the power cut, all the food in our fridges quickly deteriorated. Our evenings were spent by candlelight and, when the few candles we had ran out, by the light of lamps improvised from a beer bottle, a strip of cloth and the oil that Craig had drained from the sump of Layland's car. They burned with a putrid smell and blackened the ceilings above us. We went to bed early, nine o'clock at the latest, and soon found ourselves going about our business exclusively between sun-up and sundown. We could no longer cook at home, all our stoves were electric, and we ate communally at the barbecue pit that had been dug in the square outside Dave's. Our supply of canned food quickly dwindled and these evening meals consisted almost exclusively of rabbits and boiled Brussels sprouts, they being the only vegetable that Vito could still successfully grow. The week after the power was cut we turned on our taps to find them dry: they'd cut the water too. We collected up old bathtubs and sinks, rummaged around for plugs to match, set these up under the cut-off downpipes of our houses and prayed for heavy rains. Though (on the day after the shooting) Alex had quit his job, joined our ranks, demolished his hut, moved in with his mother and brought the bulldozer inside the wall, the trucks still continued to arrive at the tip and without Alex to spread and bury it, the pile soon grew into an enormous rotting mountain of waste whose unbearable stench wafted across *ur* on the breeze. The stray dogs moved out there to scavenge for food at night and howl execrably into the morning on the far side of the wall.

By the time winter came around again and almost three months had passed since Layland's arrival we had still heard nothing from either government or shire that would either confirm or deny his news. Far from being the insurance policy we had thought him to be, it seemed in fact that to his employers Layland was completely expendable. No-one had come looking for him, nothing stirred outside the wall; the written assurances that Michael was demanding looked no more than a barren hope. Food was now almost non-existent, sanitation had deteriorated dangerously; Layland's wound had become infected and Marie-Claire was growing increasingly concerned about it. She had been a nurse in Paris, and was now visiting Layland daily. She eventually relayed the gravity of her concern to me via Craig, probably the better to avoid involving Michael. Craig reiterated his own concerns, not only about Layland's leg but about the whole sorry situation, and in turn made a radical proposal. He would take the car into town, he said, buy the necessary medicaments for Layland and spend what cash was left on supplies. I argued against it, but Craig won me over in the end. He saw no danger—We've become paranoid for no reason, he said—but to satisfy my concerns and avoid any unnecessary discussion with the others he would sneak out under the cover of darkness, shop first thing in the morning, hide out in town and return the following night. I made up a bed in the spare room for Marie-Claire (she wouldn't sleep in Craig's house on her own), we waited until after midnight, then Craig and I pushed the old car out through the gate and a little way down the access road. I handed him two hundred dollars in cash, wished him luck, went back inside and closed the gate behind me. All was quiet. I gave the prearranged signal then hurried back across the square towards home. I heard the car start up and above the wall I could see the faint glow of the headlights in the sky. Marie-Claire and I talked in the kitchen for a while, a halting exchange in broken English, before she went off to bed. I sat alone at the table, unable and unwilling to sleep.

Craig had only to turn the headlights on to see what he was up against and said later that he was tempted then and there to give the whole venture up. Halfway down the access road a grader had been parked, blocking it completely. It had probably been there for months. Craig turned in off the road to the left and tried to cut across the paddocks on the far side of the tip, intending to skirt around the grader and join up again with the access road near the highway. But in the dark he lost all sense of direction, became completely disoriented, and found himself driving around in circles unable to regain his bearings. Eventually and without warning he suddenly drove straight into the creek at almost forty kilometres an hour; the car became bogged to the axles and wouldn't move another inch. He tried to dig it out with his hands, knee-deep in stinking mud, but the task was beyond him and he trudged around the paddocks for another hour in the dark, mud-bespattered and weary, before he finally arrived at the South-West Wall. He followed it back to the gate and arrived at my house at three in the morning, a dishevelled, stinking mess. I poured him a little of the brandy I'd saved and gave him a change of clothes. I checked the pockets of his old clothes—he'd also dropped the wad of money, somewhere out there in the mud. All was quiet the next day in *ur* as the meaning of this latest disaster gradually sank in.

Weeks passed and still no-one came. We frightened away the dogs and scavenged what food we could from the tip. One afternoon a herd of cows gathered at the gate. We let one in and slaughtered it in the square and ate what we could of it over the following week until the meat went bad and had to be buried in a pit outside the wall. Months passed, then one morning we heard a light plane flying high overhead before receding into the distance. The following day it returned and as it came in low this time over *ur* a plastic-covered parcel was pushed from the door. It fell onto the roof of a house in West Street and broke open on the lawn: ten cans of baked beans, ten of sausages and vegetables, six packets of dried peas and six of instant potato. We had no idea who was behind it but that night we made a meal of it anyway and ate like hungry wolves. Two days later the plane came again, this time with twenty bars of chocolate and a packet of flour which broke open and scattered on impact and in the end proved unsalvageable. The drops continued then at irregular intervals and they became our main source of food. Alex insisted that they were coming from the farmers up north—sympathetic to our cause—and we did our best to believe him. But in the end it mattered little from whence these gifts had come, what mattered was that they came at all and were saving us from starvation.

One day, I remember, a parcel fell in my backyard and I stared at it for a long time from my kitchen window before I finally hurried out, gathered it up and brought it inside. I opened it up on the kitchen floor: it was all I needed and more, I thought, for a clandestine dinner for two. I invited Jodie over the following night. We ate the contents of the parcel, cold, at my kitchen table, and said hardly a word to each other all night. As she stood at the front door, ready to go, I put my hand on her shoulder. Jodie, I love you, I said. Her lips turned up into a grimace or a smile, I still don't know which, and she turned and walked out into the dark.

nine

If you have ever walked into a musty room, a room shut up against a long cold winter that is now finally drawing to a close, and caught the sweet perfume of a bunch of flowers, the first flowers of spring, you might have some idea of the air of freshness the three visitors carried with them into *ur* that day and why we responded to them so amiably. We'd had no forewarning, they simply turned up at the gate. The one in the suit and tie, Loch, called out to Vito picking sprouts in the square from the few miserable stems that remained; the other two, dressed in blue uniforms and caps, stood with their hands behind their backs a little off to one side. Loch asked to be allowed in, he was from the city and had business to discuss. The news swept through *ur* and within minutes everyone had gathered at the gate. It was an overcast day after a week of rain, muddy puddles lay everywhere around, and I remember gazing at their shoes, which looked so clean and shiny, thinking: We must not let them get dirty. Loch's first concern was to see Layland; once that was done there was nothing that couldn't be discussed. We opened the gate and escorted them across the square. Though the two in uniform averted their eyes officiously towards the ground, I could see Loch's gaze wandering over the scene of destruction around him. Our little village, our sweet little piece of suburban paradise, had become an inglorious shambles. Rabbits hopped about everywhere and their droppings littered the ground; weeds cascaded from the gutters of the houses and moss covered the roofs; rubbish from parcels that had shattered on impact lay scattered about everywhere: tin cans, cardboard packaging, plastic wrappers, broken bottles—on rooftops, in driveways, front yards and backyards and in the barren patch of wasteland that had once been the square. I hung my head, in shame, I suppose, not daring to catch the visitors' eyes, and followed the group to Michael's house lagging deliberately behind.

Layland's gangrenous leg was gone. Marie-Claire had performed the operation with a carving knife and hacksaw and Layland had suffered it uncomplainingly, knowing death to be the only alternative. He sat in his usual armchair in the darkened room with a blanket over his lap. Little could be offered to the visitors by way of refreshments but a fire was hastily lit, a weak pot of tea was made and someone ran back to Dave's to get the packet of chocolate biscuits we'd saved, perhaps without fully realising it, for just such an occasion as this. Loch carried a letter from Layland's wife and there was a deep respectful silence in the room as Layland opened and read it. He placed it delicately in his lap, bowed his head and quietly wept. The tea was poured, the biscuits handed around; the clink of cup on saucer was the only sound for a while as we all drifted off into our own private thoughts. We still had no idea what the visit was about but we had become so used to bad news that I suppose we were all taking this moment to prepare ourselves for the worst. It was a chance to reflect also, and I reflected back on many things during that seemingly interminable silence, leaning in the doorway, my head sunk on my chest. I looked up for a moment and caught Jodie's eye, the briefest glance; there was no sympathy, no forgiveness in it. She remembered well enough my talk of high ideals, grand hopes and new beginnings; her look impaled me for an instant to those hollow words then burst them like an arrow to a hot air balloon.

Loch introduced himself and his two companions, Alan and Geoff, and apologised for making his visit unannounced; there had been no way of getting a letter to us, and besides, he'd preferred to approach us personally. If we'd been silent up till then, the next fifteen minutes held us so speechless that I wondered as it drew to an end whether any of us would be capable of uttering an articulate sound again. Loch had come to offer his apologies, we had been inexcusably forgotten, various shake-ups in the department for which he now worked had meant that attention had sadly been diverted to other projects and if various and apparently unrelated things had not brought our case to his attention we may well have been forgotten altogether and forever. The first was a letter from Layland's wife; as Layland himself was now fully aware she had for some time been living with another man but with all the best will in the world she couldn't completely discard him from her memory. After a series of phone calls had gone unanswered she became concerned and wrote to the department in the hope of having his whereabouts clarified. This letter should have been acted on immediately; unfortunately it wasn't, and he, Loch, had only just come across it last week. Around the same time a new employee joined the department, a former real estate agent whose expertise was to be used in a couple of other housing projects that were currently on the drawing board. Over lunch one day, and purely by chance, this new employee,

Robinson by name, had asked how the old *Outer Suburban Village Development Complex* was going and had the plans for its destruction been carried out? You may remember him, he lived here for a time. (Dave's jaw had dropped and his eyes glazed over; I raised my head and looked towards him, suddenly realising who Loch was talking about.) Well, continued Loch, it was a strange collusion of events: I went back to the office and looked through the file. Now correct me if I'm wrong but my understanding of the situation is this: you have all lived here for just over eleven years now and as far as I can see your reason for staying has been based on a promise which our department had originally made to build a freeway out here in order to reduce commuting time and expand your job opportunities; an indispensable promise, to my way of thinking, given the distances involved. However, for reasons which still escape me at this stage this freeway was delayed, all the other residents left, you stayed, but not without making your disappointment known. You were consequently offered some form of compensation (I'm still not sure of the details) which you duly accepted and which has apparently been deposited into a joint bank account on a monthly basis and has been your main source of income since. All very well, I don't think any of us have a problem with that. But at this point the story seems to take what I can only describe as a bizarre turn. According to my records—and they are somewhat sketchy and erratic here, I grant you—some fifteen months ago, over the course of six months, some hundred or so houses were suddenly destroyed by a group of as yet unidentified vandals who had stolen the bulldozer from the tip overnight (and I'll get around to the tip in a moment) in order to wreak their havoc. Fortunately all of these houses were unoccupied and no injuries were suffered, but the damage, as I imagine it, must have been substantial. To give you my personal view of things here, I find this entire scenario totally incomprehensible and cannot find words sufficient to express my outrage at the fact that the situation was allowed to deteriorate to such an extent that vandalism on such a massive scale as this could even be possible. We are talking about government property here after all—as you know, when the freeway was delayed, all the houses except your own were bought back by the government and as a government employee the wilful destruction of these houses must be my chief concern. But I am also aware that lives too were at stake. Our neglect in this regard was indefensible, and the fact that you subsequently took matters into your own hands causes no problem with me. However, I will need to have one or two things clarified here—this is partly the reason for my visit—for it appears that immediately following this wide-scale vandalism a collective decision was made to protect yourself from any further incursions. It also appears that this decision resulted—rightly or wrongly—in the building of a wall. Well and good. But I don't think anyone could stand outside this wall and look in at us gathered here in this house today without feeling that there is something decidedly wrong with a system that has driven a group of otherwise ordinary citizens to this end. I am shamed by it, speaking personally, ashamed to be a part of this system and an instrument of it. It's a remarkable wall, don't get me wrong, more amazing by far than even rumour had suggested, and its construction is perfectly understandable under the circumstances, but it does raise serious questions. How could this be allowed to happen?—is the first question, of course, but more than that, now that it has happened: What are its implications and where do we go from here? Well, my department's response, as you well know, and to be blunt, was callous in the extreme. Your monthly compensation payments were stopped, precisely at a time when they were most needed, and your bank account summarily closed. It is enough that we shirked our responsibilities in this time of crisis; by any bureaucratic standard it is deplorable that government property was allowed to be destroyed without any action being taken to prosecute the offenders or prevent it happening again, but it is simply beyond me to understand how this order could have gone out to abandon you to the dogs, so to speak, precisely at a time when our assistance was most desperately needed. I am looking into the matter, you can rest assured on that. And what of Layland here? I make no excuses for him. I hold him accountable as I do all those involved in this matter, but there is the old saying about shooting the messenger and I can't help feeling some sympathy for him. The fact is he was following orders—an age-old excuse for all manner of evil, I agree—and though I understand the dilemma he was placed in it is still a disappointment to me, knowing what I know now, that he couldn't see fit to follow his conscience instead. He was the first outsider to visit here in years, he more than anyone should have seen how misguided the department's decision had become concerning matters of which they quite obviously had little first-hand knowledge. You have paid a heavy price, Peter, but I feel compelled to say it is a price you had to pay. Of course his message is absurd in the extreme, I have no doubt that you recognised it as such straight away; I am yet to lay my hands on the perpetrator but when I do he'd better have a good story ready. There was never any plan for a satellite town, much less a plan to build a one-hundred-kilometre stretch of freeway, the cost of which, by my calculations, would consume two and a half times the department's current budget. Quite the contrary in fact: since the failure of the OSVDC—you don't mind me calling it a failure, I'm sure; we're speaking not as enemies here but as friends—the department's thinking has shifted so far away from such types of planning as to make them seem almost a joke. (Yes, it was a joke, I might as well say it now.) We simply cannot afford to think along these lines any more: expansion and more expansion, a continual 'looking out', the idea that every inch of empty space should be considered useless unless filled has lost all popularity now and rightly so. The OSVDC, of course, was seen at the time as some sort of compromise between the two alternatives, expansion on the one hand and contraction on the other, but like all compromises it was doomed to failure from the start. Set it over fifty kilometres out of the city, in the emptiest space you can find on the map, give it meticulously calculated proportions and for want of a better word call it a village, but know that the instinct for expansion is irrepressible and that in time this village itself will expand to fill the empty spaces around it. I wonder where the planners' heads were at when they devised such an intellectually satisfying but completely impractical plan. They believed in it, of course, I don't deny them that, they bought up all the land around the OSVDC at the time on the strength of their belief and honestly expected that within the year, buffered by a narrow green belt, new suburbs would grow as if by magic on the outskirts of their village. Well, you all know how that ended up. Within two years they were trying to sell the land back to the farmers from whom they'd bought it but the farmers, quite understandably, I think, seeing the land so radically devalued by having a housing complex slap-bang in the middle of it, would have nothing to do with the idea. The shire stepped in, as you know, acquired a ridiculously good bargain, used a portion for the new rubbish tip they'd been planning and leased back the remainder to any interested farmers they could find for a hefty profit. So that's what became of these 'innovative' planning ideas; back then, when such ideas seemed to my horror to pass into legislation unquestioned, a satellite town such as Layland here obediently carried news of might indeed have been put forward as a valid proposal and, God forbid, might even have been built. But I can assure you such wild suggestions would not pass unquestioned now. Contraction, I'll stake my reputation on it, contraction is what will save this country from its woes. Who wants to walk three blocks to visit a neighbour any more when you could talk to them from a balcony across the way? Yes, I'm of a European cast of mind myself, and it's to that continent and to their sense of space and proportion, their refinement of the notion of contraction into a way of life, that I turn for my inspiration. The OSVDC was an experiment, well and good, and I'm not denying that it had something of the European in it, the village, I mean, but it was a compromise and no experiment based on compromise can hope to yield useful results. The city is where we must now concentrate our attention, the city *is* the centre and no matter what science or art or other intellectual discipline you are working in, the centre must always be your starting point and the source of all your thinking. Very well, you say, but where does that leave us? In a precarious position, I grant you. These are the new planning ideas—I've explained them briefly, and perhaps too cursorily—and whether we like it or not they have made the old ones redundant. However, as you may or may not have gathered, I am not about to hoist the department on the petard of pure theory, we have a practical responsibility too, and it is to this—over the past week and in the light of what I've heard, read and seen here today—that I wish to now turn my mind before advancing our charter of high-density living any further. The short-term problems are now the most pressing. I understand that a group of farmers, sympathetic to your plight, have been supplying you with food, but a quick glance around convinces me that, for all their good intentions, these supplies have been inadequate. Letters have already been sent to them, individually, thanking them for their efforts but insisting that this duty will now fall again to us, as it most certainly should. I've already spoken to your bank manager in town and upon the chief signatory—who is that?—upon the chief signatory filling in the necessary forms a new account will be opened and immediately credited with, well, a not insubstantial sum. In the meantime I have with me in my car a number of items, food, medicine and the like, that may be of some use—Alan will get them in a moment. So much for the short term—if there's anything else, please let me know before I leave today—but I'm afraid we must now turn to matters of a more delicate nature. Certainly, two sugars. I have laid my cards on the table and perhaps in a roundabout way offered my apologies on behalf of the department for the way these matters have been dealt with. But while I hold a superior position in the department I am not able to operate outside its normal democratic processes. So far as I am concerned the wall can stay; it is yours, you built it, and I don't doubt it cost you a good deal of labour. But I'm afraid many others in the department take a less tolerant view than this. They don't doubt it was built for a purpose and as a consequence of our own neglect but they now believe its purpose has been served and that it should come down. Further to that—please understand these are the views of others, not mine—and without making too big a thing out of it, there is a generally held view that, in a free and democratic country such as ours, a barbed wire–topped wall in any context must be seen as an inappropriate thing. If we are to resume our support, and I sincerely hope we can, then I can only say that in my opinion greater sympathy will be given to a housing complex without a wall than one with. It's a delicate matter, I agree; I don't broach the subject lightly. You must understand that one sees things differently from the outside; to you the wall is protection and perhaps even aesthetic improvement, to the majority of those in the department it is both an easily misread symbol and an eyesore. I have taken this matter in hand myself and will give you certain assurances now: firstly, the wall can come down in your own time and at your leisure providing it be within twelve months of your agreement to do so; secondly, you need have absolutely no reason to fear the vandals again, the two gentlemen with me here, Alan and Geoff, are employees of a reliable security firm contracted to us and will stand guard as of today on a rotating shift and, bolstered further when the wall comes down, will continue to stand guard until such time as we all, in agreement, have satisfied ourselves that the threat has subsided; thirdly, if and when the wall comes down, we will guarantee to remove all the remaining building rubble at no cost to yourselves and have, indeed, a sub-contractor on standby at this very moment for the purpose. I don't expect an answer straight away, Alan and Geoff will stand guard at the gate tonight and will be ready to relay your decision to me the moment it is made. And now, if you don't mind, I'd like a quick word with Layland. His position needs to be clarified and I believe he would prefer that it be done in private. Thank you all for your attention, and again, on behalf of the department, I offer my heartfelt apologies. The future is in your hands; we will offer what assistance we can but the rest is up to you. I hope the estate can survive, it goes against my theories, obviously, but if the ultimate test of any idea is its persistent continuation in the face of overwhelming odds then I believe you have already and decisively proved this small circle of earth to be worthy of a bright happy future.

We left Loch and Layland alone and filed out of the lounge room onto the front porch where we all stood, stunned and silent. The sky had darkened; night was falling. We stood there without speaking for a long time. Eventually Loch came outside; Layland had decided to go back to the city with him. We didn't object. The two security guards carried him out, his arms around their necks. He gave us a wincing smile as he passed, asked the bearers to stop for a moment and gave Marie-Claire a kiss on each cheek then waved them on again. They carried him across the square through the open gate to the car before returning in a series of relayed trips with our boxes of supplies which they stacked on Michael's front porch.

As Loch prepared to leave, shaking everyone's hand in turn, I saw Michael furtively thrust an old dog-eared notepad in front of him—he'd taken notes of everything Loch had said—and ask him to put his signature to it. Loch flinched, momentarily, then took the pen from Michael and hastily scribbled on the final page. Michael put the notepad in his pocket. Loch walked down the driveway, smiling forcedly back at us all and offering a few final assurances before stepping quickly across the square. A few of us strolled over to the corner of East Street and watched the two guards close the gate from the outside, lock it, and position themselves on either side. Loch's car started up and began reversing up the access road with Layland in the passenger seat, staring blankly back at us through the windscreen.

We'd forgotten to ask him about the power and water. Someone tried the porch light at Michael's but it didn't work; Jodie called from the darkened kitchen that the water was still off too. Perhaps tomorrow, someone said. A couple of lamps were brought and we began opening the boxes on the front porch. They were empty, save for some cardboard packing material, half a dozen bricks to weight them and some old moth-eaten second-hand clothes. A fire was lit in the pit outside Dave's and three rabbits and two cans of beans were cooked. The gate had been left open earlier and some dogs had wandered in off the tip; they sniffed around the glowing bed of coals and cracked the discarded rabbit bones noisily with their teeth. Later that evening I walked with Jodie back across the square to Michael's house where we found him still sitting on the front porch, gazing vacantly up at the stars. He hadn't eaten. There's some leftovers in the kitchen, Jodie said: I'm going to bed. And she disappeared inside.

Look up there, said Michael: look up there at that. I lifted my gaze to the stars. He talks of contraction; look up there and tell me if he isn't talking shit. A smile broadened across his face. We'll be spreading out, said Michael, expanding, until the end of time. And we won't rest happy till we've filled all that up too. They could build a ghetto for us, stack us one on top of the other, but the fact is you either get on with your neighbours or you don't. And if you don't, and that's usually the case, you'll do whatever you can to get as far away from them as possible. There'll be estates, suburbs, towns like this sprouting up like mushrooms across the universe for the next ten billion years. I'm more concerned about tomorrow, I said. Tomorrow? Michael laughed. Ha! What's that?

Jodie called from inside for her father to get in out of the cold. I made my way back across the square. The two guards stood smoking and chatting outside the gate, the calm broken intermittently by a burst of static from their two-way radios. They nodded to me as I passed. I heard a voice raised in one of the houses behind me in South Street; it sounded like Craig's, but I couldn't be sure. I had saved a small bar of chocolate at home and ate it sitting up in bed by the greasy light of my bedside lamp. Later that night I heard a helicopter flying overhead and saw the glow of its searchlight passing by the window. The dogs started barking and continued long after the thump-thump of the rotor blades had faded into the distance. Much later again I thought I heard someone knocking at my door; I went to answer it but there was no-one there. All was strangeness that night in *ur*. I pulled the blankets up tight around me and finally slept a sleep full of dreams that would come back to haunt me again and again long after that strange night had passed.

ten

I was not a witness to the events that followed, they were described to me later, by Jodie. I had locked myself up in my house: for good, I said, forever. The following morning Vito was gone. He'd apparently left during the night, taking his meagre possessions with him; later that day his tracks were found in the mud by the West Wall and a handmade ladder was found resting against it. He'd jumped the wall, crossed the creek and was probably already halfway to Melbourne. But all this was discovered later: the main drama that morning centred around a section of the South Wall, at the corner of South Street and the old ring road. Craig and Marie-Claire had been up since dawn, they'd roused Dave and Alex too, and the demolition was already well under way. They'd begun the work without any prior discussion and by mid-morning had already opened up a two metre gap. Craig's motives were pure, however misguided; he'd hung on Loch's every word the previous night, assumed the wall to be the only hindrance to a resolution of our troubles and had woken early to apply himself straight away to the task of bringing it down. He believed, I'm sure, in his innocence, that the sub-contractors' trucks would soon be arriving to take the bricks away and in anticipation of this he had begun stacking them into neat piles a few metres apart. By lunchtime, when Michael finally arrived, they had ten or so such piles and the gap in the wall was at least four metres wide.

You would have to have been there; I wasn't, and can only do my half-hearted best to describe the scene that followed. Michael appeared marching down South Street dressed in a rabbit-skin hat and an old khaki army jacket which, as Jodie said, he'd found that morning among the second-hand clothes in one of the boxes of supplies. He was carrying his gun. At first Craig thought he was simply off to shoot rabbits—a little late perhaps but there need be nothing strange in that. Michael cocked his rifle, aimed it at Craig and told him in no uncertain terms to put every brick back where it had come from, now. Craig was speechless; he was convinced he was doing what had to be done and now Michael was telling him at gunpoint to undo it. Dave intervened, pleading with Michael to stop this nonsense: if they were going to get their subsidies back, the wall, as Loch had said, must come down. Alex chimed in: What point was there in delaying it? The sooner we send the right signal to Loch, the sooner everything will be resolved. Michael repeated his demand. The wall was staying and if Dave or Alex or anyone else didn't like it then there was the doorway to the city, go. Alex sat on a pile of bricks and dropped his head into his hands. There was a long pause then, as Dave stood staring at Michael, thinking his situation through: eleven years, mostly happy ones, a business, good friends and companionship. He suddenly turned, walked through the gap in the wall and began striding out across the open paddocks beyond. Perhaps sensing Michael's presence and more importantly the loaded gun behind him (and remembering the wounding of Layland), he broke into a run, stumbled, fell, picked himself up again and took off as fast as his old legs would carry him. Was he thinking of Slug, and the city to the south; was he running *to* or *from*? He veered south-east, weaving his way through the clumps of gorse and thistle while the group at the wall watched his slender figure recede. But way out on the paddocks Dave suddenly stopped, stood there for a long time looking south, then turned and looked back towards *ur*. He looked out across the paddocks again—What's he doing? someone said—then finally turned on his heels and ran, arms flailing, back towards the gap in the wall. He stopped about ten metres away, between Scylla and Charybdis, a look of horror on his face. They're coming, he said.

Just then the crackle of a two-way radio was heard and the sound of footsteps approaching around the outside of the wall. Dave hurried inside, his chest heaving. Michael stepped out through the gap just as the two guards turned the corner and immediately fired a shot over their heads. They turned and ran, one of them tripping headlong into a gorse bush. Michael fired again, and again, and they ran south towards the horizon that Dave had just retreated from, not even bothering to unholster their pistols. Beyond them then, on the southern horizon, the first sign appeared. A puff of black smoke, the sputter of an engine, and the vague shape of a yellow bulldozer, enormous even at that distance. It's the freeway, Dave said, still trying to catch his breath: it's just over the horizon and it's headed this way.

All that afternoon and throughout the following day no more movement was observed on the southern horizon but Michael wasted no time in preparing for the sudden charge that would surely come. The bricks were quickly relaid and Craig was sent out to check that the rest of the wall was secure. (In doing so he found the evidence of Vito's departure: the footprints in the mud and the makeshift ladder. A house-to-house search was organised but Vito was nowhere to be found.) Later that afternoon Alex drove his bulldozer out the gate, Craig riding shotgun on the step, and, starting from the spot where the old dam used to be, he began excavating a second branch of the creek southward. I heard the engine revving back and forth all day long and well into the night that followed. The idea, apparently, and I had to hand it to Michael as a good one, was to build a moat, completely encircling *ur*. The original creek, flowing from the northeast and then around the western edge, would protect us from that direction, the new branch being dug would cut around our eastern edge, cross the access road and join up again with the original in the south. *ur* would effectively become an island, surrounded on all sides by at best a muddy trickle—but an island nonetheless. In less than two days the work was complete. The bulldozer was brought back inside and parked as added defence inside the access road gate and that night, as if God had smiled on Michael's supposedly lunatic plans, the heavens opened up, the rains came down, and by morning the new moat was filled. All work stopped then, both inside *ur* and out on the rain-besmirched horizon; it poured for a week, and aside from a sentry rostered on to the South Wall everyone retreated inside and waited.

When the rain finally eased, *ur* was a quagmire; we could only hope that the paddocks to the south were too. But within a few days the bulldozers and graders, their huge steel tracks untroubled by the slush beneath them, were on the move again. Slowly, almost imperceptibly, the earth-moving machinery grew larger, cutting a wide path through the landscape towards us. From the South Wall you could see the tip trucks coming and going, ferrying the soil away, and back behind the frontline of bulldozers and graders enormous rollers chugged back and forth. Whatever tales the two guards might have carried with them in their mad dash across the paddocks that day (brick walls, a bulldozer, barbed wire and guns) had obviously been ignored and it seemed nothing could stop the advance that—without any doubt now—was closing in directly on *ur*. Each afternoon at five o'clock a whistle blew, the engines stopped and the workers trudged back over the horizon; each morning at eight they started up again. The weather had cleared—our eleventh spring was almost upon us—and more rapidly each day now the gap between us closed.

I spent most of my time sitting up in bed with the

curtains drawn listening to the vague sounds drifting in from the square. I still couldn't find the strength to face the events unfolding around me. Then one night—I was standing by the sink, unable to sleep, gazing out of the window into the dark—there was the sudden muffled sound of an explosion. Michael, Craig and Alex had begun blowing up the earth-moving equipment. Alex had kept a stash of gelignite from his days with the shire council; with blackened faces the raiding party of three had crossed the paddocks, laid their charges and were now igniting them, one by one. Jodie pounded on my door and pleaded with me to come down to the wall. I threw on some clothes and followed her across the square down South Street. Alex's bulldozer was parked hard up against the wall with the bucket raised, and sitting high up in it, with a clear view of the paddocks beyond, were Dave, Nanna and Marie-Claire. I climbed up to join them and gazed out in astonishment at the spectacle before us. Far off in the distance two bulldozers were already burning; in the foreground all was dark, then the red glow of a lit fuse could be seen creeping in and out of the gorse bushes and suddenly, with an almighty thump, a third bulldozer rose up off the ground and exploded in a ball of red and yellow flame. In the light given off by this explosion I could then see the three dark figures scurrying to the next fuse; again the tiny red glow dashed through the bushes and again, another explosion. They blew up three bulldozers, two graders and a roller that night before returning to *ur* triumphant and adjourning to Dave's to toast their success. I stayed up in the bucket with Jodie, Nanna and Marie-Claire—I would not go down to the square—and for a long time we watched the fires burning against a backdrop of moonless sky.

I fell asleep in the bucket that night with Jodie in my arms. Never have I felt such warmth, such bliss. As dawn broke across the paddocks and we awoke, untangling ourselves and rubbing the sleep from our eyes, the aftermath of the night before was revealed to us in all its horror. Most of the machinery was still burning, belching clouds of black smoke up into the air; police cars and fire trucks had gathered with their blue and red lights flashing, and uniformed figures could be seen standing about in small groups as if trying to come to terms with the carnage around them. As I crawled back into bed later that morning, alone, the smell of Jodie's hair still lingering in my nostrils and the sound of her soft breathing still in my ear, I knew it was only a matter now of waiting for the end, an end more certain than ever after the events of the night before.

A few hours later a megaphone was heard addressing us from the other side of the South Wall. It was Slug: he was standing, alone, beside a white four-wheel drive with government plates. The group gathered inside the wall to listen, a brick was removed at eye-level and one by one they peered through, each turning away dismayed: Dave, the last, so overcome with emotion that he could not be moved to speak again. Slug, for motives pure or tainted, was acting as emissary and arbitrator, a last-ditch attempt to bring those inside around to reason. We were deluding ourselves, he said, and had acted precipitately; the earth-moving equipment behind him which we had so savagely rendered immobile the previous night had not been out to harm us and it was beyond him to understand what had inspired us to such an act. Were we all mad? Couldn't we see that the freeway that had been promised to us so long ago was finally coming? What had possessed us to try to stop it? It hurt him deeply, he who had worked so tirelessly since returning to the city to draw attention to our plight and had tried, finally with some success, to turn the rusted wheels of bureaucracy in our favour. Our houses had already doubled in price (he had buyers standing by with chequebooks in their hands); within a month we would be linked to the city as promised, the petrol station would be built, new houses added, shops, factories, warehouses, the park would be landscaped, the lake dug and filled; by summer at the latest all the details of the original plans would be realised and improved upon. He was asking us only to take stock, stop and think, and show a little patience; he'd lived among us, knew what we'd been through, if we couldn't trust him who could we trust?

No-one believed a word of it, but the gall of the man held the small group inside the wall in a stupefied silence. Michael climbed into the bucket and asked Alex to raise him up. The others put their heads together to peer through the hole in the wall. I was not one of them but it brings a smile to my face even now to imagine the look on Slug's face: he, in suit and tie, standing behind his shiny white four-wheel drive, looking up to see cockeyed Michael rising above the wall, his face unshaven, his left eye wide and wild, the rabbit-skin hat on his head and the old army jacket buttoned to the neck. They looked at each other for a long time; in quiet tones Slug pleaded with Michael personally to stop this madness, it wasn't worth it, and would all lead to disaster in the end. From his pocket Michael drew out the notepad that Loch had signed, supposed proof of an entirely different scenario to the one Slug had just outlined. He held it up in front of him, read it through aloud, tore out the final page, shoved it in his mouth and began chewing it up. Then, with one quick snap of the neck, he spat it out in Slug's direction. The wet ball of paper landed at Slug's feet; he picked it up and began prising it open. Don't bother, said Michael, it's full of lies; as you, Slug, are full of lies. He shouldered his rifle and fired. The bullet hit the ground at Slug's feet; Slug dropped the megaphone and jumped into his car. Another bullet ricocheted with a ping off the roof as he turned it around and drove at full speed back across the paddocks. Michael gave the signal to be lowered. He dismounted and told Craig to go out and fetch the megaphone: they'd find a use for it before long. He then helped Dave to his feet and whispered something in his ear. Dave smiled, Michael put a hand on his shoulder and together they made their way down South Street to the bar.

New machinery was trucked in over the days that followed and within a week the freeway was moving again. Two police vans now accompanied the advancing bulldozers as protection against another raid; they did not try to talk us out—if Slug had failed what hope did the police have?—but their presence out there was a sobering reminder of how far the situation had deteriorated. As night fell and the workers left for home, a spotlight on top of one of these vans was switched on and its beam slid back and forth across the open ground between us. I sometimes crept out to the wall after dark to watch this beam and to see how far they had advanced that day: Alex's bulldozer was now parked almost permanently at the end of South Street and the hoist and bucket served as a mobile sentry post with a commanding view of the paddocks beyond the wall. I sat up there with Craig, Dave, Alex, Nanna, Marie-Claire or Jodie—with anyone, in fact, but Michael, who I now did my best to avoid—and talked or simply watched in silence as the spotlight passed back and forth, sometimes freezing a rabbit in its beam.

But despite our forebodings, the progress of the freeway was proving to be painfully slow. We had expected the excavations to reach us first before any bitumen was laid but it seemed in fact that the work was advancing piecemeal: the earth-moving equipment would stop for a while and then behind them the gravel trucks and spreaders would do their work before the excavations advanced again. It seemed to indicate a hesitation on their part and suggested—to me at least—that the end might not be as swift and decisive as we'd first imagined. As for Michael, his behaviour became increasingly reckless and bizarre and I did well to keep out of his way. It seemed that the strain of waiting for the final moment was taking its toll. He spent most of the day at the wall with the megaphone in his hand shouting abuse across the paddocks and was often seen running down South Street after dark in his pyjamas, suddenly concerned that they may have moved in the night. He organised a working bee to barricade the access road gate with whatever was at hand, junk that had been scavenged from the tip mostly, and topped the wall again with more barbed wire and broken bottles. In the midst of all this he seemed completely unaware of the fact that the freeway had almost stopped, or was crawling so slowly now that it might as well have stopped, and acted as if they were already on our doorstep when in reality they were still over a kilometre away to the south and hardly moving at all.

In the eleventh summer after Inauguration Day dear old Nanna died. My only regret, and it is a regret I'll carry with me to my grave, is that I did not speak to her over those last few days. Jodie had knocked at my door in the morning and called me down to the wall. Nanna's out there, she said. It was the first time I had ventured outside during daylight hours in over a month and in the meantime the freeway had begun moving rapidly again. A lone worker had spoken to Alex late one night as he stood guard at the wall. The workers, he said, had been deliberately slowing the freeway down, reluctant to be the ones responsible for ploughing through our homes. But their bosses had become wise to this and were now threatening to bring in the scabs. Within days the freeway had leapt forward again and covered more ground in an afternoon than it had in the previous week, and as I looked through the peephole in the wall at the end of South Street that morning the first thing that struck me was how close they now were: less than three hundred metres away and closing fast. But the real shock was Nanna. She sat with her back to us, her face to them, in front of the enormous bulldozer at the head of the column. She was still dressed in her blue nylon nightie and held a small posy of flowers in her hand. She went over the wall last night, Alex whispered to me: I couldn't stop her. Extra police had arrived, their cars parked higgledy-piggledy around her, and some kind of negotiations were in progress. It was hard to follow what was happening; we could hear nothing at that distance but the occasional crackle and static-drenched voice from the police radios and everyone crowded and pushed around the peephole for a look. Michael was up in the bucket, megaphone in hand; he'd been shouting abuse and giving ultimatums all morning. Two policemen tried to lift Nanna up, taking one thin feeble arm each, when Michael suddenly shouted through the megaphone and fired a shot into the air. They lowered Nanna down again. A police megaphone shrieked out a warning to Michael; Michael in turn abused them with a list of unrepeatable words. It's been going on like this all morning, Alex said: that's my mum out there, what am I going to do? The negotiations began again but Nanna was unmoved. Suddenly the bulldozer coughed into life and above the sound of its engine the police megaphone could be heard: We will now pull back and I would ask you to do the same. Some of the police cars turned around and retreated to the end of the column. I have no doubt they were sincere, that the driver of the bulldozer had meant to put it in reverse, but alas for poor Nanna the best intentions mattered little. The bulldozer lurched forward, there was a shout from one of the policemen—No! Back!—but it was too late and within a second Nanna had been crushed. The driver finally found reverse and backed the machine away to reveal Nanna's body lying twisted and lifeless on the ground, the posy of flowers still in her hand. Alex, screaming, tried to scramble up the wall and had to be physically restrained while above us Michael began firing wildly and the sound of bullets ricocheting off metal filled the air. The police grabbed Nanna's broken body and retreated behind the bulldozer. Hold your fire! came the cry through the police megaphone. Michael kept shooting until his magazine was empty. Then all went eerily silent.

This event, so senseless in itself, sparked a chain reaction that threatened to get completely out of hand: there can be nothing so mad as the madness that followed. We never saw Nanna's body again—an ambulance whisked it away that afternoon—but if, as I believed, they were trying to cover up the death and the whole fiasco *ur* had become then they didn't entirely succeed. News somehow leaked through to the town up north and the consequences were swift and dramatic. The following day 'reinforcements' arrived (I'm aware of how stupid that must sound but can find no other word to describe it): farmers mostly, driving tractors, and a group of council workers (Alex's mates, as we later discovered) all crammed into the cabin of a bulldozer. They parked their machinery outside the South Wall in the path of the oncoming freeway. Later that same afternoon it began raining food from the sky. All day every day during the days that followed, the light plane flew again overhead and dropped food parcels into *ur*; they thumped and broke open on the ground so often that it became almost dangerous to go outside.

I do not know what was behind this sudden outpouring of support—since Loch's visit the food parcels had stopped and we'd had no contact with any of these people for years—and it seemed to me an extreme overreaction at the time. But food was food, and for the first time in months we ate civilised meals again. No-one could say how long this glut would last or when the freeway would carve its last three hundred metres into *ur*; for a moment we forgot all the goings-on outside the wall and spent most of our time eating. People took to their homes again: Craig and Marie-Claire spent the days inside, sharing perhaps for the first time and in deliberate defiance of the shambles around them the lifestyle Craig had promised; Jodie came to my place every night for tea and by the light of an oil lamp on the kitchen table a vague hint of the romance I'd longed for was revived; Alex disappeared into his dead mother's house and was rarely seen again; Dave, bless his soul, from the day of Slug's appearance at the wall, had taken to sitting as many hours a day as Michael would allow at their old table on the footpath outside the bar and now, after scavenging among the food parcels scattered in the square, ate his meals there religiously, wrapped in a nostalgic dream. Only Michael, like some prowling animal, roamed the streets with gun in hand, chewing at most on an old rabbit bone, his mind completely gone.

If we could have held that moment, frozen it in time, shut out all the sights and sounds that suggested disintegration and ruin, we might yet have believed in our dreams and seen long, contented lives ahead of us. More than ever now, and against all rational thinking, with Jodie sitting across the table from me of an evening, I wanted to turn the clock back and start the story all over again: this is my wife and this is the meal she has cooked; soon her eccentric father will drop around and I will tolerate him, as I should, and ask him to come with us to the park on Sunday where with our two children hand in hand we'll cross the grass to the lake and throw crusts of bread to the ducks. This is my wife, this is my home, my children are sleeping and all is well with the world. They were saying that now, out in the east, but how far away it seemed!

eleven

The stand-off outside the wall continued; the freeway was temporarily halted. Michael roamed the streets and the inner circle of the wall by day and slept in the bucket of the bulldozer at night. He still had Craig's support and he (Craig) now wore his own hastily made rabbit-skin hat as a sign of his loyalty but everywhere else the solidarity that Michael had previously enjoyed was eroding. Alex remained unsighted, Dave sat at his table all day long and only rose from his chair every hour or so to wipe the neighbouring table with a piece of cloth, as if acting out at intervals a memory from long ago. He should go inside, Jodie said to me one day: it's too dangerous now out in the square. It was true, he should have gone inside, but neither I, nor Jodie, nor anyone else for that matter thought to go out there and talk him in. Food parcels fell like meteorites now, so regularly they had become almost meaningless, and the day after Jodie's prophetic words one fell on Dave's head and killed him. He was buried in the square, beside the bronze plaque that for God knows what reason still remained where it had been erected over eleven years ago; an old beer bottle filled with flowers was shoved into the dirt at the foot of the grave and that was the end of Dave. Michael went berserk; he fired at anything remotely associated with 'the murderers'; the farmers with their tractors and the council bulldozer fled under fire across the paddocks and when the plane wheeled overhead again later that day Michael emptied fifteen rounds in its direction and we never saw it again. He expended the last of his ammunition from the South Wall that night, shooting blindly in the direction of the freeway until the last bullet was spent.

Later that night he knocked at my door and we spoke for the first time in months. Jodie and I had just finished dinner and she, sensing the delicacy of the moment, tactfully offered to clean up while Michael and I talked in the lounge room. Her hope, I'm sure, was that I might somehow save him from himself. He was an awful sight, a shadow of the tanned and wiry outdoorsman of so many years ago. He hadn't shaved for weeks and now sported a rough, grizzled beard. He had lost weight—Jodie had tried and failed many times to get him to eat. Beneath the ugly beard his face was thin and pale, his clothes were dirty and dishevelled and if not for the fire still burning in his eye and his nervous, twitchy movements you might think him a man sinking inexorably and uncaringly towards death.

All day a storm had been brewing to the west of *ur* and that night thunder and lightning racked the sky, rattling the windows and filling the air with the smell of rain. Michael's raw nerve ends were doubly raw: he jumped at every clap of thunder and turned to the window, eyes blazing, each time a flash of lightning lit up the sky outside. It was all I could do just to get him to sit still in his chair, he wouldn't look me in the eye: it was impossible to say what disturbed him more, the storm or me, but then his demeanour changed, he laid his hands gently on the armrests, sat back, looked up at the ceiling and closed his eyes. Bram, he was saying, do you have any idea how ridiculous all this is? Of course you do, that's why I haven't seen you for a month. He opened his eyes and pinned me with the left in a hard, sardonic gaze: but never start something you can't finish, that's all I can say. Jodie! he shouted, come in here! She walked into the lounge room, drying her hands on a tea towel, and stood calmly in the doorway. I want you both to know that I approve, said Michael, and not only do I approve but I give my blessings, unconditionally. I won't deny that it's been a struggle for me; after everything that's happened, Jodie, I know you'll understand. He raised his hand, removed the rabbit-skin hat, and placed it carefully on the armrest of the chair as if to emphasise the gravity of the moment. It was the first time the hat had left his head in months; his greasy, greying hair was stuck flat to his skull and made him look sadly comical. I began my time here with so many hopes, he said, like so many of us, running from an unhappy past to a new and unknown future. When Jodie arrived—sit down, Jodie—when Jodie arrived the better part of my hopes were realised. I had my daughter with me again after a long and agonising separation—you know, Bram, that I was making my preparations and was on the point of leaving when this happy event occurred. This suburban dream is not for me, I said, the house is too big and lonely; but then you came, Jodie, out of the blue, back to your father, and everything inside me changed. It's true, by then this place had already gone to rack and ruin and anyone with any sense had well and truly left but I had my daughter, I had *family*, and this was enough to convince me to stay. Life was suddenly filled with good times, times I'd forgotten existed. We went out shooting rabbits again like we used to when you were small—do you remember?—at that magic hour after dawn. But you're no longer small, you're a woman now, and I'd be the first to admit it's taken some time for me to accept that fact. I've forgotten how true love works. I've forgotten many things. When I first mentioned the wall to Bram he didn't try to stop me (though I knew he thought the idea was mad) and it wasn't until some time after that I realised why: he was nodding his head out of love, love for you, Jodie, and yes, sometimes true love is as unfathomable even as that. Jodie turned on her heels and walked back down the hallway to the kitchen. I could feel myself turning red. She's embarrassed, Bram, it's understandable, said Michael: a father shouldn't embarrass a daughter like that. Jodie! Please! Come back a moment. (I need to talk to you alone, Bram, too, and I will before I go.) Jodie, please...His bottom lip began quivering and his hand passed vaguely across his face. Jodie stood again in the doorway. Your father has become ridiculous, Jodie, I know that. I know how I must look. But please, be patient with me, I'll say my piece and then I'll go and leave you both alone. I only want what's best. Michael's chest heaved and he began to weep. Jodie sat on the arm of the chair by the door and gave me a brief, impatient glance. Dave and Nanna, he blubbered, so senseless, so cruel—he took out a filthy old handkerchief and blew his nose—I still can't believe what has happened. And Alex too, you can be sure of that, he's tried his best for his mother's sake but soon he'll be gone and I don't blame him. He folded the handkerchief into his lap and tried to compose himself again. He looked up at us both, his eyes still glistening with tears: So what's left to fight for now, you ask? Craig is like a son to me, you both know that, but do you know how much it hurts me to see his dreams reduced to this? To have to try and explain every night the gulf between his long-distance promises to Marie-Claire and the daily reality of life in this place? Marie-Claire—with one exception—is without a doubt the most patient and suffering woman I have ever met but she shouldn't have to suffer for *nothing*. Craig offered her a house, a backyard, a new life in the estate north of Melbourne—I do what I do for Craig and Marie-Claire too, you mustn't forget that, but above all, Jodie, Bram, I do what I do now for you, for your future happiness, for all that I fought against in myself before, as a father, a perhaps too-loving father, for your life together, the kind of life I so miserably failed to achieve with a woman who truly never loved me—yes, Jodie, never—and who would not take my love, a love that I then transferred to you, my daughter, and which has blinded me to the thing that I now see before me so clearly, namely your love for Bram, his love for you, and your justifiable disdain for a father who has loved so selfishly and without a thought to the independent woman you've become.

Jodie returned to the kitchen, I could hear the dishes crashing in the sink then the sound of the back door slamming. I sat speechless, unable to move. Already the storm had broken and the rain was falling on the roof. I looked at Michael and saw for the first time that he was mad. It all rushed forward at me, everything, a blinding flash of clear-headedness. Michael was mad, had already led us into the most inexplicable madnesses and was about to take us even further. I stiffened, something soft and electric-like released itself into my gut. Michael pulled his chair up closer to me. He stank: his clothes, his skin, his breath. He leaned forward and cocked his head to one side, the madman's look of disarming sincerity in his eye. So you see, Bram, he said, the important thing is that no matter what the cost—two houses, two homes, yours and Jodie's, Craig and Marie-Claire's, must be saved. Forget everything else, it must be simplified to this: two couples, two homes, in which two families can be raised. It may be a long shot, Bram, but I'm prepared to do everything in my power, make any sacrifice, to achieve this one, simple and, I now believe, achievable goal. He leaned further forward and lowered his voice into a conspiratorial whisper: But I need your help, Bram; this is my plan. The wall won't hold. It's a good wall, a fine wall, but it just won't hold. We have to reinforce it. There are about a hundred unused houses left; tomorrow I will go to Alex and ask him for one last favour. If he can demolish even half these houses for us before he leaves we will have enough bricks to build another wall inside the one we've already got; if they break through the first we still should be able to hold them at the second. But if they manage to break through the second they will be virtually into the square. Of course, I'm counting on them giving up before then—I believe we've already worn them down—but if it comes to that we must have somewhere to fall back to. This is what I propose. He leaned back in his chair. Imagine, if you will, when the bulldozer bursts through the second wall with a column of advancing machinery behind it, expecting to find a place of ruin and rubble inhabited by a few miserable souls with rags of clothes hanging from them and the spark of life long gone from their eyes—well, of course they would not hesitate to drive their freeway through it. But then imagine if instead they found this: two neat suburban houses with a common back fence, clipped lawns and newly planted shrubs and flowers, a husband in each front yard with a hose in his hand and in each backyard, chatting over the common fence, two wives with newborn babes in arms. Now tell me if on seeing this even the most heartless worker could continue the charge? This is what I want you to turn your mind to, Bram, I will take care of the second wall but if you can see that vision within it then I want you, I beg you, to do what you can to turn it into a reality. Now, he said, I've said my piece. There's only one last thing. You'll soon be married, you and Jodie, my only child. I don't know where I'll end up after all this is done and it doesn't really matter but this may be the last time we speak together. You think I'm mad, I know that, and chances are I am. But never think your father-in-law was mad without reason: I want you to have this. From beneath his jacket he pulled out an old leather satchel and handed it to me. I could feel myself resisting, saying: No, I don't want to take it—but then, inexplicably, something in me melted. I held out my hand and Michael solemnly put the satchel in it.

Jodie took him home that night and put him to bed. After the momentary calm and clarity—for a moment he *almost made sense*—he flew off again into a series of wild ravings, called for his gun and vowed to go out and attack the invaders that instant in the name of Jodie, his daughter, his son-in-law, Bram, and the grandchildren for whom he'd already found names. My own mind was an uncontrollable brew of indignation and terror. I prowled the house, unable to sleep, eventually threw an old blanket over my shoulders and walked out into the rain. I walked the ring road inside the wall five, maybe ten times round and came back home again drenched to the skin. I sat at the kitchen table with the leather satchel in front of me. I sat there for a long, long time. Finally, I opened it up and pulled out the bundle of yellowing papers. I picked up the first, and held it in front of my eyes:

BLUEPRINTS FOR A BARBED-WIRE CANOE

Be sure you're sick of life; say to yourself: I've had enough. Take a roll of rusted barbed wire and some pieces of nail-infested wood and shape it into a canoe. Choose a moonless night, a night with no moon, the darkest night; you are the only witness, the only one who should see. Take your canoe down to the filthy creek when the stench is at its worst, tighten the chin strap of your hat and button your jacket up hard—the journey will be long and fraught with danger. You will use no paddle, you will need no paddle, but will carry a big jar of salt with you and throw handfuls from the stern. This will propel the canoe away from the dark unfathomable ocean, of which the salt is a cruel reminder, upstream towards the pure crystal waters at the source. Recite the prayer 'Nothing Matters, I Don't Care' three times every hour: this will give you strength. Hold your head up high. Never doubt the wisdom of your journey, do not ask Where or Why; the canoe is a sensitive one, it may turn on a pinhead and rush you back to the ocean or drop like a stone beneath you. All night you will travel and well into the following day. When the salt runs out do not despair, the waters will be clearing now and the canoe will know it has safely left the muck behind. Dip the empty jar over the side and hold the contents up to the light; you are looking for water so clear that it seems not to be there, that the jar itself appears to dissolve in your hand. If you do not find it on the second day, do not despair, go on, if you do not find it on the third, repeat the prayer more often and hold your head a little higher. If you do not find it on the fourth or fifth, don't worry, go on. If after a week the jar does not dissolve and the water in it is still putrid and thick, take heart, go on, the second week may yet see you safely to your journey's end. When in the third week the canoe starts leaking, bail it out, be brave, go on, and when in the fourth week you find yourself becalmed and feel it slowly sinking beneath you, bail harder, keep faith, don't worry, go on. It is then, and only then, as your carefully thought-out and well-constructed vessel sinks slowly towards the muddy bottom that you may allow yourself to cry out: Help! But do it softly, don't make a big show of it, you are the only witness, the night is moonless again and you are miles away from home; do it softly, sweetly, and as the waters engulf you don't whatever you do forget to keep your head held high.

This was followed by a series of sketches of the canoe in question, each time adding a little more detail until it looked less like a canoe than an enormous ark, more fitted to journeying up the Amazon, the Nile, the Danube or the Ganges than the tiny creek, say, a stone's throw away on the other side of the wall. I turned the pages, one by one, until I finally turned to the last: an enormous vessel that whole families could have lived in, a floating city that would never float. I put the bundle of papers together, tapped them on the table, and slid them back into the satchel. I then sat at the kitchen table for a long while listening to the rain outside. Later I heard the sound of a bulldozer starting up and the crashing of bricks from the direction of the South Wall. That's it, I said. I carried myself slowly to bed, blew out the lamp and lay quietly thinking in the dark.

twelve

Michael didn't even get a chance to ask for Alex's help in fulfilling his wild new scheme—the demolition of the houses and the building of a second wall—for by morning Alex was gone. Some time during the night, it must have been about two or three a.m., he'd started up his bulldozer, lowered the bucket and driven it straight through the South Wall and the swollen southern section of the creek across the paddocks towards the gathered mass of machinery. The tracks it left scarred in the soft ground were like pointers conveniently laid down for the oncoming freeway. I woke late that morning from a night-marish sleep and the place was already abuzz. Michael and Craig were trying to repair the broken section of the wall, while out on the paddocks the day's work had begun and the freeway inched closer again. Jodie and Marie-Claire took refuge in my house in North Street, well away from the commotion; I went down to the wall for one last-ditch attempt at talking Michael into reason. He didn't listen; the rabbit-skin hat was pulled down hard over his ears and he continued slapping mud onto bricks and handing them up to Craig. Craig threw me a glance, understanding but reproachful, as if saying: Help us repair the wall, Bram, otherwise get out of the way. I left them to it, returned to North Street and told Jodie and Marie-Claire to gather together whatever they might need for a quick and easy escape. I threw some things together myself, the few worthwhile possessions I had, and shoved them into a suitcase that I left in the hallway by the door.

Just after midday that day the freeway suddenly lurched forward—there's no other way to describe it. Within the space of an hour the front-line bulldozer had pushed its way to the creek and crossed it and was within metres of the wall. Michael and Craig managed to patch the hole that Alex had made but their work was hasty and slipshod and as fragile as a house of cards. Throughout the afternoon the other bulldozers and graders drew up behind and stood just over the other side of the creek: an enormous, throbbing, threatening mass of machinery. Michael and Craig worked frantically to reinforce their work, dragging up old building rubble, furniture, bedding, uprooted shrubs and anything else they could find. As evening fell and the threat momentarily subsided, Craig returned to my house to check on Marie-Claire, leaving Michael camped amid the pile of junk, presumably planning his next desperate move.

I could hardly look Craig in the eye, so infected had he become with Michael's madness. I offered him some food—it seemed he hadn't eaten for days—and left him alone in the lounge room with Marie-Claire while Jodie and I sat glum and silent in the kitchen. The two couples, I thought, that Michael, now standing guard on the last line of defence in the last hours left, was prepared to give his life for. Craig, in his ridiculous hat, mud-spattered, starving and weary, and his fiancé, from Paris; me—a fool even unto myself and tired of the farce my life had become—and Jodie, concerned, as I knew, with nothing but her father's rapid descent into lunacy. It was we four who were soon to be chatting over our back fences with the smell of fresh-cut grass and freshly washed nappies in our nostrils, we who within the confines of a brick and barbed-wire wall would live, work and procreate in some tiny suburban idyll. These thoughts were suddenly interrupted by a knock on the door: it was Slug, he'd returned, a haunted, troubled look on his face. They're coming tonight, he said, you have to get out: where's Dave? I ushered him down to the kitchen, he nodded to Jodie, almost embarrassed, and took a chair at the table. Dave's dead, I said, they killed him with a food parcel. Slug put his head in his hands and wept; tears streamed down his fat rosy cheeks, his bottom lip blubbered up and down and small drips of saliva fell from it onto the table. What do you mean they're coming tonight? I said, but Slug wasn't listening. Where is he buried? he asked, between sobs.

Jodie and I helped Slug to his feet and we walked together out into the square. Yesterday's rain had cleared and the sky above us was filled with stars. The night was balmy, still and warm. Jodie and I supported Slug as he stood at the foot of the grave, his head lolling on his chest, rocking to and fro. The flowers we'd placed in the beer bottle had withered and died, they were little more than dried stalks and brown petals now and lay limp with their heads on the ground. Where's Nanna? asked Slug, softly: I'd like some flowers to put on the grave. She's dead too, I said. He burst into tears again. We walked across the square to the few tables and chairs that still stood on the footpath outside the bar. Moss had begun to grow in the hollows of the seats and the tables were covered in a thin film of green slime. I wiped down three chairs and a table and went inside to the bar. Everything was covered in cobwebs and dust and a thick musty smell hung in the air. I searched the three fridges and the crates out the back and finally found an unopened bottle of Dave's old home brew. I took off the cap and brought it outside. There were no glasses: we drank straight from the bottle, passing it back and forth between us. Slug finally calmed down, enough for me to give him the details of Dave's death and ask why he, Slug, had returned. He drew a deep breath, held out his hand for the bottle and took a long swig. They'll come through the wall tonight, he said: most of South Street will be gone by morning. I couldn't live with my conscience any more, I've come back to help you all out and do whatever I can to set you up with a new life elsewhere. You've only got to say where you want to live, pick your house and I promise I'll get it for you, each and every one of you, on very reasonable terms. My car is parked outside the North Wall, I've arranged with the pub in town to provide rooms for the night—no-one else will know you've gone or where—and if you know what's good for you you'll get what things you need and go now.

For my part I had not the slightest hesitation, though I was sure Jodie would not be so easily convinced. Then suddenly, as if on cue, we heard the sound of an engine coughing into life from the direction of the South Wall. We ran back to my house as one by one the other engines started up. In the lounge room Marie-Claire sat alone on the couch, quietly weeping; Craig had gone back to the wall with Michael, to make the final stand. Jodie swept Marie-Claire up into our group before she had a chance to think—Jodie herself, it seemed, had suddenly and irrevocably made her decision—and we fled up North Street to the wall. We clambered over it, with the help of bits of timber laid up at an angle, and scrambled down the other side on the plank Slug had left there earlier. I was the last up, the others were already throwing the suitcases and boxes into the back of Slug's four-wheel drive when I saw Craig running up North Street towards me. So he's changed his mind too, I thought, and waited until he arrived, breathless, at the bottom of the wall. He was carrying a crate of empty beer bottles and I remember thinking: My God, how deeply Michael's madness has touched him when the only thing he can think of taking with him is that! But then he called up to me: Petrol, we need petrol, ask Slug can we have some petrol? I didn't know what he was talking about: was it some residue of an ancient hope dashed years ago—the petrol station, the subsidies, the dream of a car on the freeway to town? Then I realised, he wanted to fill the bottles with petrol, the last weapon they had now that Michael's ammunition was gone. We looked at each other for a moment. Please, Bram. One last favour. For Michael's sake. He held out a short piece of garden hose and pushed it towards me.

Craig came up over the wall and Jodie and I filled the bottles from Slug's tank—I could read her thoughts, but she didn't dare speak—while Slug sat silently waiting in the driver's seat, knowing better than to interfere. Craig and Marie-Claire stood off to one side, saying a last goodbye. I caught his words, his voice raised for a moment above the distant sound of the engines: I'll be with you soon, don't worry—then something in French that I didn't understand. He climbed back up on top of the wall, I handed the crate of bottles up, then he waved goodbye and was gone.

Slug turned the car around and we cut across the paddocks, through the new eastern branch of the creek and the empty paddock that used to be Vito's garden, bumping up and down over the old irrigation channels, past the now abandoned tip on our left and the rusting grader still parked on the access road to our right and finally out onto the bitumen and to the highway north. I sat in the passenger seat; Slug drove silently, his thoughts far away; in the back seat Jodie cradled Marie-Claire in her arms and watched the dark paddocks and barbed-wire fences flash past. We drove down the deserted main street into town and pulled up outside the pub. The publican—I vaguely remembered his face—was standing on the front steps, hopping from one foot to the other, ready to greet us.

It was well after eleven and the public bar was dark and quiet as the motley group filed inside. To anyone's eyes we must have looked a sight. Our clothes were ragged and dirty, our faces pale and thin; I hadn't shaved or cut my hair for months. The publican—Ted—showed us all upstairs where two rooms had been prepared: one for Craig and Marie-Claire (which Marie-Claire entered, alone), the other for Jodie and me. They had obviously not been used for years, but mingling with the must was the strangely alien smell of fresh linen, scrubbed porcelain and the heavy scent of pine room freshener. There was one double bed against the wall. They'd put a few clothes in the cupboard for us—they reeked of mothballs and were completely ill-fitting. Jodie had first shower in the bathroom down the corridor; when I returned from mine she was sitting at the small table by the window dressed only in an over-sized t-shirt, her hair still wet, her skin lit by the fluorescent streetlight outside. Ted the publican knocked, and brought in a complimentary bottle of cheap champagne. He and Slug were having a drink downstairs, he said, and we were welcome to join them if we felt up to it. In the meantime, drink this, it's on the house. The champagne glasses felt so light they could have been made of air, the clean taste and the tingle of bubbles on your tongue was like drinking mineral water straight from a mountain spring. It took less than five minutes for the sight of Jodie sitting by the window in the strange silver-violet glow of the streetlight with a champagne glass in her hand and her wet hair streaked across her shoulders and back to completely overwhelm me. The room spun for a moment and then, finally, I was holding her in my arms.

That night, back in *ur*, Michael and Craig prepared to make their final stand. Unbeknown to us Michael had corralled some horses off the paddocks into a backyard in West Street; he selected the two fittest looking beasts, gave them rope bridles and reins and had them ready and waiting in the square when Craig returned from the North Wall with his supply of petrol-filled bottles. They each lashed a crate to the side of their horse, gave all the bottles rag wicks and stacked them into the crates. The plan was to break a small opening in the West Wall, ride out in a wide arc south-west and attack the advancing column from the rear. I can't imagine what possessed Craig to agree to such a foolish scheme, and, as he related all this to me later, he was still unable to explain why he had submitted himself to it. They knocked out just enough bricks at the end of West Street for the horses to pass through and rode out a little after midnight under the cover of a moonless night. But the plan was doomed from the start: the freeway had advanced too far now to be stopped, and, by the time Michael and Craig had ridden out and crossed the creek on the western edge the bulldozers were already crashing through the South Wall. The riders circled wide in the darkness, the bottles rattling in their crates, only to find that most of the machinery was already inside *ur*. They managed to hurl one flaming bottle at a huge roller still parked on the south side of the creek, then Craig dropped the box of matches in the dark—they searched but couldn't find them and beat a hasty retreat. They rode back towards the gap in the West Wall, now planning to somehow stop the column as it came down South Street to the square, but Craig's horse lost its footing in the creek and all his bottles fell from their crate. He stood knee-deep in mud, trying to calm his struggling horse, and watched as Michael rode through the gap down West Street, hooves resounding on the bitumen. He called out to him, urging him to retreat, but Michael didn't hear. That was enough for Craig; he finally extricated both himself and his horse from the mud and rode like a madman across the paddocks towards town.

I was asleep, entangled in Jodie's arms, when Slug knocked loudly on the door. I followed him downstairs;

Jodie still lay sleeping; Craig was sitting at the bar next to Ted with a blanket draped over him, clutching a glass of brandy. He was covered in mud from head to toe, his beard and hair matted and stinking. I sat beside him and laid an arm over his shoulder. He gave the details of the past two hours in a halting fashion, stopping occasionally to sip the brandy, sometimes staring blankly into the glass for a minute or two while he gathered his thoughts again. He had no idea where Michael was now—kept saying: But I *had* to go—whether he had ridden into the square and probable death or had retreated safely somewhere, who knows where: where was there left to run? He asked after Marie-Claire and I told him she was sleeping; he turned to me, looked me in the eye, and in a soft voice said: We have to go.

All was a flurry of activity then: Marie-Claire was woken and told to pack, Craig showered and changed, Slug offered to drive them to the airport and drank two cups of black coffee to try to sober himself up. I pulled Slug aside and in a quiet but determined voice demanded that he give Craig and Marie-Claire the money they'd need. He was too shocked to refuse. I'll fix it all up at the airport, he said. With their bare belongings Craig and Marie-Claire were hustled out the front door of the bar down the steps into the dark and into Slug's waiting car.

Jodie came down wrapped in a blanket, still rubbing the sleep from her eyes, to say a last goodbye. We watched the car drive off down the main street until its two red tail-lights blinked and disappeared.

We went back up to bed; I couldn't sleep myself and sat for a while at the table by the window. I took the old leather satchel from my suitcase and put it on the table in front of me. I gazed at it for a long time, transfixed, but I couldn't bring myself to open it. I turned towards Jodie; she seemed to be asleep, her hair spread out like tiny rivers on the pillow. I left the satchel on the table and crept quietly downstairs.

The bar was quiet and deserted; one dim light shone above the spirits' shelf. I walked around and poured myself a brandy. There was the sound of a door creaking, then I saw a light come on in the Saloon Bar next door. The door opened and a stocky, thick-set man came in carrying a mop and bucket. The cleaner, I thought; is it that late already? He nodded to me silently, stood the mop in the bucket and leaned it against the wall, then began stacking the chairs on the tables. Big night, he said, without looking up. Yes, I said, and we both fell silent again. The story is that most of it's already gone, he said. He was talking about *ur*. How do you know? I said. Spies, he said, then looked up and smiled. And Michael? He got away, they don't know where—mind if I join you? I didn't have the chance to answer; he moved across the room and sat on the stool directly opposite. I suppose the taps are off, he said: well, I'll have a brandy too. Like an obedient barman I poured him one and placed it in his hand. Yes, there won't be anything left by morning, he said: I've got a mate who drives a dozer, he was in town a little while ago to buy some takeaways for the boys. But don't worry about Michael, he got away, and I'm sure it won't be the last we'll hear of him either. Smoke? I shook my head. So what happens now? the cleaner continued: your guess is as good as mine. Do I wait again, on another promise, or give up all hope of going back to my trade and stick with the mop and bucket? I didn't know what he was talking about but was too tired and confused to ask. Of course, there'll be another promise, he said, you can bet your boots on that, but I don't know whether I can believe them any more. You've got to know when to give up hoping, that's the art of happy living, so far as I'm concerned. Which house did you live in? At the end of North Court, I said: I moved to the corner of North Street and the square after Michael built the wall. Yes, I would have worked on them both, the cleaner said: I worked on all the houses up there. I had two labourers and an apprentice, you know; a thousand bricks a day we'd lay, just our gang alone, we'd knock over a house in less than a week. Hah! What a time that was! We thought the work'd never end—we had no reason to doubt it. This was just the start, they said; they'd bought up all the land around, when the freeway came there were going to be another two hundred houses added and once that was done, well, there was no telling where it would stop. I don't know what happened. We were a real little community in the town here, the tradesmen waiting for the expansion of the estate; I've lived in that room up there, just down the corridor from yours, for almost fourteen years. Then, well, just like that! Bricklayers, tilers, plasterers, plumbers, electricians—oh yes, we were a real little community back then—up they got and off they went. Tony, they said, give up, mate, there'll be no more work out here. They're building a freeway out in the east, they said; that's where you want to be. I had some good mates, among that crowd, and maybe I should have listened. But can I tell you something about me, Bram? I'm a dreamer, that's all. No, I said, I'll stay here, the freeway will come out this way eventually and I want to be here when it does. And bugger it, why shouldn't I stay? I'd moved around enough already—a little work here, a little work there—and once you've had a taste for the kind of work the estate gave us it's hard to give up the dream that there's more of the same to be had. So I stayed: Ted's looked after me, he gave me this job in exchange for a room and a little cash in hand. But it's hard, you know: look at these hands. Are these the hands of a bricklayer? Housewife's hands, that's what they are, softened by too many mops and buckets. I'd have given anything to have helped you out with that wall, you know, just to feel the roughness on my skin again, but I couldn't interfere, it wasn't my business, and I kept well out of the way. I spoke to Alex about it once, it was at that table over there: Keep out of it, Tony, he said, don't poke your nose in where it's not wanted. (I'd have made it double thickness though, Flemish bond with alternating headers—but that's neither here nor there.) And now the freeway's arrived. Fourteen years I've waited and it's finally arrived. And if it's heading north-west to a satellite town twice the size of the estate as they say then I'll need to be ready, won't I?

The door from the Saloon Bar opened and a light went on: it was Ted, in an old woollen dressing gown. So what about doing some work now, motormouth? he said: we open in a few hours' time. Goodnight, Bram, you should get some sleep. He flicked off the light and disappeared again. Tony put his empty glass on the bar and gave me a conspiratorial wink. He's a good boss, he said, and yes, I'll probably be working here, emptying ashtrays and mopping floors until the day I die. But we all need our little dreams now, don't we? He finished stacking the chairs and began rhythmically mopping the floor. All was quiet. I watched him for a while—Tony, the bricklayer-in-waiting, probably the most deluded of us all—drank another brandy then climbed the stairs to my room. As I reached out for the doorhandle I suddenly hesitated for a moment, and for a moment a most magical image passed across my mind. Tony would build a house for Jodie and me, a beautiful house, brick by brick, somewhere out there on the paddocks where the estate used to be and we would live happily ever after in it with our brood of children who would procreate down through the generations and build other houses, one by one filling all the gaps in the empty landscape until between fence and fence, neighbour and neighbour, there were no more gaps to be filled. As I entered the quiet, half-dark room and hung my shirt on the back of the chair the first thing I noticed was that the old leather satchel was no longer on the table. Then I turned to the bed and saw that Jodie was gone.

thirteen

There were all kinds of rumours, it became impossible to sort fiction from fact. But from the scraps of stories that came back to me I was able to build up some kind of picture of the period following the destruction. I stayed on in my room in the pub on my own and had plenty of time to work on this picture and add the extra touches it needed. A slight exaggeration here, some extra drama there; it mattered little to me now how much of it corresponded to the truth. There was nothing I could say to compete with the wild versions that circulated each night in the bar. The only ones who could tell you what really happened over the months that followed were Michael and his daughter and they, in their separate ways, are both far gone now and way beyond asking.

Michael rode down into the square that night as the bull-dozers moved up South Street, taking the houses with them. But he had not gone down there to make a final stand, as Craig had thought; even in his madness he had more sense than that. Instead he dismounted at Dave's, tied up his horse, ran to the gate in the East Wall and ripped bits of timber and barbed wire from it. He dragged them back to Dave's grave in the square beside the plaque and hastily built a fence around it. What meaning there was in this I couldn't say, but it was Michael's last act before leaving *ur* for good. He untied his horse, remounted and galloped off down West Street through the gap in the wall. I must have been down in the bar with Tony when Jodie sneaked out by the back door of the pub into the carpark that night for her rendezvous with Michael. Did I hear the hooves on the bitumen? Perhaps I did, I'm still not sure. They rode off together into the night.

For over a month Michael wreaked havoc in every country town within a fifty-kilometre radius of *ur*; any office which was in any way connected with the government or shire council could not hope to be spared his merciless revenge. Every night, while back in their bush hideout Jodie kept the campfire burning, he rode into another town, threw bricks through windows and daubed slogans on walls. People caught sight of him, the strange figure in the old khaki jacket and rabbit-skin hat, galloping down the main street with his heels digging hard into his frail horse's flanks. It might have been a dream—how many people told themselves on crawling back into bed that it *must* have been a dream?—but in the morning as they arrived at the post office to buy a stamp, the town hall to pay their rates, the local Member's office for a chat, they were quickly shocked back into reality. Mad Michael had passed by in the night and the evidence of his wrath was clear.

Rumours of his exploits spread, and though people began speculating wildly on the reasons for them, no-one but the cognisant few ever managed to connect the story back to the destruction of *ur*. And as much as you might admire Michael—and many, many did—in this sense his adventures proved to be a complete failure. He believed he was making a point, but amid the chaos, the panic and the fear, the point was completely lost. No-one had a yardstick to measure such fervour by, and certainly no-one in their wildest imagination could trace the violence back to some vague notion of a house, a family and a happy life in the former housing estate north of Melbourne. He carried a grudge, obviously, against certain government and shire instrumentalities, but who doesn't occasionally carry a grudge of this kind, even if their method of unburdening themselves of it may be somewhat less dramatic? Or perhaps he was simply an escaped lunatic and there was no method in his madness at all? Everyone had their theories and their own particular reasons for holding them but no-one *understood* Michael, and this lack of understanding only rankled him all the more and drove him to deeds that even further defied the most carefully applied logic. He began attacking *other people's houses*, the new brick veneers that were always cropping up on the edge of country towns. A newly married couple would arrive with their furniture and all their hopes and dreams ahead of them only to find every window smashed and slogans painted in the driveway. He raided real estate agents, housing finance companies, lawyers who handled conveyancing, furniture shops, hardware stores, anything to do with houses or housing; one night he torched a whole building supplies yard and reduced it to smoking ash. Whatever sympathy he may have enjoyed began to quickly evaporate as almost everyone in some way or other came in contact with his unbridled ire. His days were numbered and he knew it; he spun in ever-decreasing circles, eyes everywhere for the knife that would soon surely take him from behind. Jodie stood by him, administered to his needs and kept them moving from one place to another in a complex series of camping and decamping manoeuvres. But she was tired, had already become ill and began each day vomiting into the nearest bushes; her admiration for her father remained unshaken but her patience was wearing thin. How long could this madness go on?

The only sympathisers they could still rely on were a network of farmers who, having formed a growing resentment towards suburban expansion in any shape or form and who somewhat misguidedly interpreted Michael to be a rebel farmer intent on stopping the insidious spread of housing into traditional farming districts, consequently took him on as their standard-bearer and spokesman. Michael was not to know all this, Jodie chose not to tell him, but she quickly took advantage of this network of support. They slept out in sheds and bungalows, were kept supplied with fresh milk, cream and eggs, and by using these sympathetic farms on a rotating basis were able to carry on the rebellion and survive. If the farmers invited them into their houses to dine with their families, Jodie would ensure that Michael ate his dinner quietly (thus doubling the mystique) while she thanked them all on his behalf, insisted that they would carry on the struggle against this haphazard housing expansion until the bitter end and let them know in the subtlest way possible how much her father valued their support. By this means they were able to remain on the run while forgoing only the most extravagant creature comforts. With rare exceptions they slept in warm comfortable beds, ate fresh and healthy farm produce, were able to exchange horses as required and keep one step ahead of the law. Michael chose his target, Jodie mapped out the quickest escape route to that night's safe haven, journeyed ahead to the farm in question (leaving Michael with a detailed map) and prepared the way for his arrival. Town by town, farmhouse by farmhouse, they crisscrossed the countryside, Michael wreaking havoc while Jodie held the fort, their notoriety increasing by the day.

The local police had made Michael their number one priority but they found him a wily quarry. With the help of Jodie's careful planning and studious use of the sympathetic farmhouses, they remained always one step behind. The best they could do was to fill out another report of the damage he'd inflicted, file it away with the others and hope that sooner or later he would make a wrong move and stumble unwittingly into their arms. He'd become an embarrassment, not only to the police but to everyone in any way connected with government or shire. On top of this and to make matters worse a new support group had sprung up and taken on Michael's cause as their own. It was inevitable, given the special place that rumour has in the life of country towns and the ease with which it can be carried, like a dormant seed, along the network of roads that connect them by truck drivers, delivery men and the forever roving sales representatives of farm machinery firms. Beginning from the town to the north of *ur*, where almost everybody was au fait with the real motives behind Michael's exploits, the true story slowly spread. Far from being against housing expansion, and acting as the agent of a handful of selfish farmers, he was in fact protesting against the scant attention paid to it and the timidity with which government and shire had approached the problem up to now. His acts of destruction were symbolic and not meant to be destructive in themselves; he wanted to draw attention in the most dramatic way possible (all other means had failed) to the tardy treatment he and his neighbours in the now failed housing estate had received. The support began with an understanding few and soon grew to a large and righteously indignant mob. They exchanged information back and forth among themselves, printed leaflets and posted them up in shop windows, and traipsed the countryside searching for Michael in order to offer their support. But he remained as elusive as ever. They began clashing with the farmers, often violently; the farmers responded in turn with a violence all their own. Soon the police were spending as much time trying to keep the two factions apart as they were in trying to track down Michael, who for the most part remained blissfully ignorant of all this and continued on his merry way.

But these new advocates for better and affordable housing were a formidable force and their claims on Michael were convincing. Soon his network of safe houses among the farmers began shrivelling; they were often physically ejected out through the farm gate, and were forced to sleep out in the open again and eke out a living by theft and beggary as best they could. They may have turned to the housing advocates, but the fact was they'd never met one and didn't even know they existed. As to why the farmers were now ejecting them, they preferred not to think too much about it. Jodie herself had always assumed that that particular honeymoon would be short-lived, given that it was based on a misunderstanding—as almost everything involving the rebel pair now was.

By this stage Jodie was four months pregnant and her enthusiasm for their fugitive way of life was rapidly waning. Often in their hide-out at night, under the stars, with the tired horse tethered a little way off (they'd been unable to replace it and it was showing the strain) and the two resting with their backs to logs and their feet to a small smouldering fire, Jodie would find herself trying to talk some reason into her father or at least open up certain previously closed topics for discussion. Sometimes it seemed as if a light breath of sanity passed across Michael's face then and he listened intently for a while. They talked about *ur*, the friends they'd made, the possibility of the satellite town being more than a rumour and the prospect of perhaps one day living there. It stilled Michael somewhat, to talk like this; beneath the soft blanket of nostalgia his fire was momentarily quelled. Often, and unthinkably before, on nights when a raid had been planned, he would excuse himself with the lameness of his horse, a moon too bright to ensure a clean escape, a headache or a grumbling in his gut, and sit with Jodie instead by the fire talking about their days back in *ur*. A simple meal was cooked, a billy of weak tea was brewed, and the talk drifted from one thing to another as the coals glowed red between them. It was too much for Jodie to expect to talk her father around to a complete change of thinking; she dared not, for instance, make light of his sense of injustice or his thirst for a fitting revenge, but she managed to calm his spirit a little and had reason to hope that before the baby inside her was born they might have put this squalid life behind them. Michael, for his part, was given time to reflect, something he'd allowed himself little chance to do before: I don't believe he had a change of heart, far from it, in fact, and would not for one moment have wanted to disown his hot-headed acts back in *ur* or his even more hot-headed acts since, but I imagine that around this time a small sense of their *absurdity* may have crept into his brain by the back door and troubled his sleep at night.

Beyond the light of the campfire, across the dark paddocks of farms, in towns known to those in the city only as names on maps, the fire lit by Michael was already raging out of control. Demonstrations and sporadic acts of violence were being constantly organised in his name. I no longer understand any more the intricacies of those days: there was something about housing, that we should all have a house, and on the other hand something about open space and clean living, the right to walk across the landscape unimpeded by the ugly growths of civilisation. They fought their battles above my head and I understood little of the noises they made. One thing I know, though, is that the freeway we had tried so long and hard to stop, and which had recently crashed so barbarically into *ur*, was suddenly halted in its tracks while the arguments about it and all things associated with it raged on unabated. It had barely passed halfway through *ur* before the bulldozers fell silent: the cruel irony of too little too late. The whole thing had become a morass of embarrassment and with Michael—pariah to more causes than could be counted in a day—still on the loose somewhere in the countryside the police were powerless to do anything about it. They knew that Michael's capture and trial was the only way to end the imbroglio he'd unwittingly unleashed and as each day passed they turned their minds more intensely to achieving that heretofore elusive goal.

I was still living in the pub in town, on the charity of various friends and strangers. I don't know what faction these strangers belonged to, or if they belonged to any faction at all; I accepted their charity with thanks but otherwise I kept my mouth shut. I assumed them to be supporters of Michael, in one way or another, who mistakenly saw me as his right-hand man and therefore a friend to their interests. So it came as no surprise to me that one night, a little before closing time, Patterson, the local police sergeant, came in and drew me aside for a chat.

He'd seen it all, old Patterson, had watched the estate come and go and was the first out there on the paddocks the morning after Michael, Craig and Alex had bombed the earth-moving equipment. His ordinary policeman's mind was still unable to grasp how the whole affair could have got so out of hand, but I suspected him to be sympathetic and determined now only to patch up whatever differences remained and return the town to the sleepy hamlet it once had been. Bram, he said to me, there are more rumours going around these days than I can poke a stick at. Most of them I wouldn't bother giving the time of day to but one of them bothers me. They say you are in contact with Michael and encouraging all this lunacy. They say—all right, it's only a rumour—that this has all been planned from a long way back; that you're looking to see the estate reconstructed, that you saw its failure from the start and made it into such a shambles that it had to be destroyed so that you could then whip up all this support to have it built again. It may be only a rumour but I have to say it makes a lot of sense. But if it's not a rumour, if it's true, listen to me, Bram: it won't work. They've got a plan to capture Michael; I can't tell you what it is but it will all be over within a week unless he's made to see the error of his ways. If you're in contact with him, as they say, do me a favour—do him, Jodie and yourself a favour—tell him to stop, tell him to hide out somewhere until it all dies down; it will all be over in a week if you don't. I could feel twenty pairs of eyes staring at me from the far end of the bar. I lowered my head; Patterson lowered his, and cocked his ear sideways. I mumbled under my breath: I'm not in contact with him and even if I was I wouldn't warn him.

The sooner he's caught the better as far as I'm concerned. And tell all these people here that I'm neither his friend nor theirs. I just want to be left alone. Patterson's head remained lowered, his left ear still cocked, as if waiting for further explanation. I stood up, downed my glass, and walked upstairs to my room.

That was the last of my involvement in the 'Michael affair'; strangers no longer bought me drinks in the bar and banknotes were no longer slipped under my door. Occasionally Ted would put a free beer in front of me; Alex, who was now back working at the tip again (transferred to its original site), sometimes wandered in after work and we shared a glass or two in silence; Tony, the bricklayer, often brought a can or two up to my room late at night; but otherwise I drank alone. The stories of Michael's capture came back to me in a fractured form; I cared little about their veracity, my only concern being that in each of the tellings Jodie got away and her whereabouts remained unknown. The police went to exorbitant lengths—it was a photo finish as to who was madder now, Michael or his pursuers. They built a mock housing display village on a small country road about twenty kilometres west of the town. From the road it looked absolutely real but was in fact constructed overnight with prefabricated sections of plywood and pine. Inside, over twenty armed policemen sat and waited. Michael rode down the road a few nights later and must have thought himself hallucinating: he'd scoured the countryside for suitable targets, had ridden this backroad many times, but had never seen this display village before or anything remotely like it. He lit a match and checked his list, turned his horse in off the road and trotted towards the first house. Every policeman behind the plywood walls stiffened and cocked his gun. Michael must have smelled a rat, for he suddenly wheeled around and bolted across the paddocks. Twenty policemen ran out of the chimeric houses and fired over his head. He cleared three barbed-wire fences and looked to have got away but his poor skinny horse couldn't manage the fourth; it hit it straight on, became entangled, bucked and struggled furiously; Michael was thrown, he hit his head on a fence post and lay tangled in the wire, unconscious.

The trial was brief and quickly forgotten. He was released on the grounds of insanity into the care of a psychiatric institution. Within days of his sentencing the fervour that had accompanied his exploits during the previous months quickly died away. No-one wanted to be associated with a classified lunatic. As for Jodie, well, her whereabouts remained a mystery. She was back in camp on the night of Michael's capture, would have waited until dawn, realised that something had gone wrong and made quick her escape. There were rumoured sightings here and there, some said she'd reconciled with her mother and returned to live in the country town of her birth, others that she'd gone to Melbourne and sought shelter under a false name in a women's refuge there, but none of these rumours could be confirmed, for all intents and purposes she had disappeared from the face of the earth and until that night three months hence her whereabouts remained unknown.

fourteen

Me? Well, I stayed on in my room in the pub in town but rarely ventured downstairs. A handful still supported me, smarted at the cruelty of Michael's capture and trial and directed their sympathies towards the only original resident of *ur* that remained. But already I was making plans to move on. Move on, did I say? Move back, rather; but it would take too long to explain what possessed me. One Sunday afternoon I asked Alex to drive me back to *ur*; he protested, of course, he more than anyone was reluctant to go rummaging around among the ghosts of the past. Drop me off on the access road, I said, I'll walk from there. We drove down the highway in silence and pulled up on the access road about two hundred metres from where the gate used to be. I'll wait for you here—an hour, he said. I closed the door behind me and walked down the road towards what used to be *ur*.

The concrete slab that should have been a petrol station was still there, now covered by creeping weeds; on my right the tip had been back-filled and the vegetation had returned. I could still see our irrigation channels, now filled with lush new grass and among the gorse and thistle a few old vegetable plants gone to seed. The sign still stood, announcing our name, but *ur* itself, that portion of land within the ring road circle, was a strange, anarchic, hotchpotch of rubble. You could see the progress of its destruction and the moment at which it stopped. The freeway itself had been abandoned: the bitumen was laid to just over the south side of the creek, then a large swathe of dirt pushed on through the square to the northern part of the ring road where it suddenly petered out. On either side of this swathe of dirt the destruction was erratic and unfinished. The entire western side of *ur* was gone, including all the shops, the supermarket, Dave's, and all the houses west of the square, but on the eastern side Nanna's flower shop, for example, still remained completely intact. East of that again a few houses on the inner circle of the ring road had only been half-demolished and even a small portion of the East Wall, just north-east of Nanna's, still stood to four bricks high. It was obvious that the destruction had advanced to a certain point—the freeway down the middle, demolition of the western edge including the wall, then preliminary demolition of the eastern side—before all work had been suddenly and mysteriously halted. The place was deserted, all the earth-moving equipment had been withdrawn, including the rusting grader that had been parked on the access road, and an eerie silence clung to the ruins and rubble.

I found an old beam to use as a footbridge across the eastern branch of the creek—the 'moat' that Alex had dug in the last days, under Michael's instructions. I laid it down over the trickle of water and passed across to the other side. A large mound of dirt blocked my path then, thrown up by the bulldozers as they carved their path north. I climbed this mound and walked down the other side onto the bare patch of ground that was once the square. A cold shiver ran through me as I realised I was standing on the spot where Dave's grave should have been: had they taken the body with them or was he still lying under my feet? I hunted around for the bronze plaque, hoping to get my bearings from it, but it was nowhere to be found. I followed the bare patch of ground north then, past where the bar used to be on my left, my second home in North Street on my right, and on past the ring road towards the creek.

There, where North Court had once been, the mound

pushed up by the bulldozers became an enormous mountain of dirt and rubble, dragged up through *ur* then dumped and left when the freeway was abandoned. I climbed this mountain to get a view of the creek and the site of my original house on the edge of North Court. It was much as we had left it, a few bits of rubble lay scattered about, the stumps of houses stood up out of the ground; the creek flowed past on its original course and beyond it the cows grazed peacefully in the paddocks. Off in the distance I could just make out the rusted shell of the car that Craig had driven into the creek.

I turned around to look south again: an extraordinary sight. From the most distant point on the horizon the freeway approached, a black ribbon of bitumen marked out in white. Then, as it neared the southern edge, the white markings disappeared, the bitumen continued, then just clayey soil, already reclaimed by the weeds, moving up through the square and North Street to finally and abruptly stop at the mountain of dirt and rubble on which I now stood. All abandoned, all pointless, useless, an ugly scar to an ugly wound. On either side of this scar the outlines of the old streets and courts could still be seen and my eye roved among them, stopping to dwell here and there on some feature that stirred something up in my memory. Why didn't it work? These streets, these culs-de-sac and all the houses in them gathered around an old-fashioned village square? But then I cast my eye further again, to the ribbon of bitumen trailing off towards the horizon, the vast flat featureless paddocks all around, and saw again the fatal flaw. They looked too far out, I said to myself, and too far out in the wrong direction.

Over the moat, way out on the access road, I could see Alex standing by his car waving his hands above his head. I held my hand up and pointed to my watch. He flapped his arms in the air, a gesture of resignation, and leaned again on the bonnet of his car. I walked down the other side of the mountain to North Court and the site of my original house. The creek flowed quietly by: the level had dropped since the other branch was dug; it was rarely more than half-full now and the water was fresh and clear—gone were the days of stinking sewage, the mud and rubbish washed down in winter. I leaned over, cupped my hands, and drank from it thirstily. A herd of cows trotted across the paddock, stood and watched me, then dropped their heads and drank from it too. It was in that moment, that moment then, that I made my decision to return.

Alex and I drove back to town in silence; he asked no questions, he didn't want to know. He lived in town now, had his job, and had put the past behind. Each

Sunday he visited his mother's grave in the cemetery on the outskirts, just down the road from the original tip, and placed a bunch of her favourite flowers on it. That was enough for him, to pay homage to her memory and mourn each Sunday her futile death; all else connected with the last days of *ur* had been wiped forever from his mind. Late that night I spoke to Tony in the bar and told him of the plans I was making. He thought me a fool, of course—What if the freeway suddenly starts up again? he said—but the desire to demonstrate to me the bricklaying skills of which he never tired of boasting was in the end too great to resist. My plans were not grand, indeed, could not be more simple; it was not even a house I wanted, just a small shack and a patch of land on the ground beside the creek. We went out the following Saturday: Tony with his trowel and plumb-bob, me with a pick and shovel. By Sunday evening we had the foundations laid and we returned the following weekend and each weekend for a month after that. The bricks and all the building materials we needed were all there waiting; we had only to rummage around for the sturdiest length of timber, the unbroken roof tiles, a window frame, a door, and cart them back to the site. The four walls went up and the roof went on; I began digging over a patch of ground by the creek in which to grow my vegetables. Tony asked for no payment;

we sneaked a few cans from the cool room in the pub and drank them together at the end of the day; that, and the weals and calluses that had returned to his hands, was all the payment that Tony needed.

It was an odd-looking thing, I won't deny it, but appearances mattered little. It all came together in the end: a rough brick shack between the mountain of rubble and the quiet, slow-moving creek. A little fence surrounded my vegetable patch, to keep the rabbits out, and a chair stood by the back door from which I watched the sunsets fade. The government was my benefactor, I was now officially unemployed. Ted gave me an old second-hand car to use—I think he was glad to finally get rid of me—and I drove it into town every fortnight to do my shopping. The days passed slowly, each morning I stood on top of the hill and scanned the horizon in the hope of catching a glimpse of Jodie, returning at last to the home I'd built for us out of the ruins of the past. But she did not come, and the days grew longer. As evening fell I walked the old streets of my imagination, greeted my neighbours, sat on a chair outside Dave's until dark, then walked my habitual walk around the ring road and back up over the hill again home. Jodie would come soon, I was convinced of that, it was only a matter of biding my time and keeping my best face on. And when she came, and she would, I would take her with me, our baby sleeping safe inside her, on that peaceful evening stroll around old *ur* until the light gave out, when we would at last return home for a long dreamless sleep enfolded in each other's arms.

I had no visitor but Tony and he would soon be gone. There was a rumour about a new housing development thirty kilometres to the west, near the town of Haranhope; it wouldn't be a satellite town by any means but he was already making plans to move there and be first in line for the work when it came. He tried often to talk me into going—I could be his apprentice, he said—but I could not be swayed. I'm waiting for Jodie, I said, and left it at that. He still thought me a fool, I'm sure, but had gradually warmed to my stubborn ways. Every Saturday at lunchtime I'd hear his car pull up out on the access road and the rattle of keys as he trudged across the paddocks around the hill to my door. We drank and talked but as evening fell the conversation petered out and the silences took over: there was nothing more to say, he was leaving soon to pursue some dream of building houses in the west that after all I'd been through just sounded like so many houses of cards. He brought me the gossip as it came to him about life in the town, the small scraps of news he thought might be of interest. Slug, he said, turned up occasionally in the bar to drink with a few old friends on his way to some new real estate deal or other and often asked after me. Tell him I send my regards, I'd say with a smile, and I hope he dies a slow and miserable death. Layland, our hostage, had apparently won a long court battle for compensation for the loss of his leg and now lived in an affluent Melbourne suburb with the wife who had so cruelly spurned him. No news of that other one, Loch, Tony would say, but you could do worse than hope he's dead. One day he brought me a postcard, sent care of the pub in town: it was from Craig and Marie-Claire. I had only to glance at it before I burst into tears. They were well and happy and holidaying in Marie-Claire's parents' house in our namesake village, Ur; the postcard showed a snow-capped peak of the Pyrenees, glistening in the sunlight. Marie-Claire had signed it with kisses, Craig's postscript was written up along the edge towards the stamp: I was going to address it to *ur* but thought it might confuse *le facteur*! Tony awkwardly put his hand on my shoulder as I sobbed and blew my nose. Craig and Marie-Claire, so far away and happy! How strange and ravelled our lives can be!

Tony left shortly after, but not before trying one last time to convince me to come with him to Haranhope. I kept the friendship open, saying: Maybe one day. We drank our last few cans together and I raised a toast to his future success. It was eight months since the destruction of *ur* and a long hot summer was drawing to a close. There was still no sign of Jodie and the days of waiting grew longer. I kept everything clean, ordered, ready; there was no telling when the day would arrive. It was no house in the east I was offering, I knew that clearly enough, but we could make our own east, here in the paddocks of the north, and live here just as happily. I say all this, and could feel it to the marrow of my bones at the time, but those last days were hard, trapped as I was between past and future in a speculative half-lived present. It was a time distinguished only by its *possibility* again, by the potential of this moment to become a more fulfilling other. How many days of my life had I spent in such a state—was it not the thing that distinguished all of life in *ur*?—and how many more days were there to come before the missing parts fell into place and the circle was complete? On the one hand there was fecund Jodie, waddling just over the horizon towards me, and on the other the ruins of our former life. She must come soon, she must, because without the breath of future she would bring with her I would be drawn more inexorably each day back into the past.

But she did not come, weeks went by and she did

not come and I began to give up all hope of her coming. This was my life now, living among the ruins. Each day I dug down into the hill of rubble with my shovel, sitting for hours in the crater I made, blowing the dust off the bits of junk I found and laying them out in a row beside me. Hours I spent among these things, piecing together small moments of our history, saying: Yes, I remember that—what a time it was! They rose up out of the ground around me: Inauguration Day and the unveiling of the plaque (here it is), the first taste of Dave's brew one warm night in the square, the strange construction in Michael's garage, Craig in the phone box (here was the mouthpiece), vegetables, rabbits, dogs, barbed wire, the wall, the siege, the food parcels falling as gifts from the sky; all these things and the stories in them lifted themselves up out of the ground each day and marched past me at night in my dreams. Every day I dug a little further down, each night I went home and made notes at my table. I stacked the artefacts up in the house and in the garden all around it: objects as signposts to memories that I struggled through the nights to record. Autumn came, and with it the rains, the hole in the hill filled up with water but I bailed it out and struggled on, dragging whatever I could up out of the mud and washing it clean in the creek. The skies cleared, then the rain returned; again they cleared, days on end of blue, I worked furiously, between hill and creek and home, with one eye always on the western horizon, no longer looking for Jodie but for the gathering storm clouds that would finally bring my work to an end.

When the rains returned they returned with a vengeance; that day the western sky blackened, the clouds were boiling heaps of buffed metal, rolling across the paddocks towards me. I gathered up my pick and shovel and retreated inside my shack. Lightning cracked the sky, thunder shook my roof and walls and rattled the windows in their frames; the clouds burst and the downpour began. I lit a fire with broken bits of timber and watched from my window as the rain swept in across the paddocks beyond the creek. Days and nights I worked then, with scraps of notes and pieces of *ur* jumbled up on the table before me as the rain fell hard on the roof. The story of *ur* had to be told; what point was there in all that had happened if it wasn't? The estate, its inhabitants, and the terrible tale of its destruction may end up as little more than a footnote in history but if I didn't write that footnote, who would? I'd given up on Jodie, the happy home, the flower-filled days of spring; mad Michael, our hero, sat in a blubbering silence in a room with white walls; the others, gone, all gone. I had little left but these straws I clutched; they were mine, I returned, I had claimed them. To hell with what anyone else might think!—they were mine, I returned, I had claimed them.

I remembered the night, but only later, much later; I remembered it among all the nights as the darkest, both outside and in. It was all very well to be trying to make out of all these fragments a sensible story for the edification of generations to come but that night, the darkest, in my yellow pool of lamplight with the rain hammering hard on the roof, it was as if suddenly all the shards had flown off to all points of the compass, smirking back at me as they went. I could no longer link one note to the next nor link a relic to that note; they remained utterly themselves, pieces, fragments, determinately unwilling to cooperate and become parts of the whole. I remember pacing around the table, saying: Something's missing, something is still buried out in the hill or still lies, unseen, on the ground. I remember my fear, a deep, uncontrollable fear, that whatever this thing was the rain would wash it from the place where it lay down into the creek and carry it away from me forever. I wanted to go outside, but didn't: the rain was like a wall of falling splinters of glass at my door. I stood and watched it and the dark night beyond. I heard nothing, saw nothing, knew nothing but that implacable fear of something slipping slowly, inexorably away.

I know what I dreamed that night because I still have it here with me, on the small piece of paper that I groped for in the dark and scribbled on hastily in the hour before dawn. It was a dream of my father, of all things, who'd died many years before. I caught sight of him passing through a dark pine forest; light rain was falling, water dripped from the trees, the ground was sodden and squelched underfoot. He passed some way off, rows of pine trees separated us, then suddenly my perspective shifted or he had turned towards me, or both, and he was walking in my direction down a pine needle–covered path between two rows of trees. He was bent over double, carrying something on his back: I couldn't make it out. Then in an instant he was passing by, without looking up or speaking, and I saw that the bundle on his back was a kind of swag, of tangled barbed wire and broken bits of wood; he had his thumbs hooked into the straps and walked past stooped and wheezing heavily. But as he passed I heard him whistling an old favourite tune: he was a good whistler, I remember that well, and a carpenter by trade. Where are you going? I called after him. He didn't stop, didn't turn and look back, but I heard his voice clearly above the sound of the rain and the heavy drops falling from the trees. Down to the creek, he said, and continued on his way. I woke from this dream suffused with warmth, the most beautiful feeling, impossible to describe. I put the piece of paper on which I'd written the dream in my pocket and swore to keep it with me forever, to remind me of that indescribable warmth, an inner glow, like a small smouldering fire, impossible to describe. And when I set about my work at the table again that morning I did so with a sudden and renewed vigour, as if all the fears of the night before had too been so many dreams, as if nothing were missing and I'd been a fool to think so and that the task of reconstructing the story of *ur* from my many and varied fragments was little more than an admittedly time-consuming formality. But I had all the time in the world, I told myself; Jodie would not be coming now, nor would anyone else, and my days alone among the ruins had only just begun.

fifteen

In the end it rained for four weeks solid. In the days following Jodie's death and my last trip into town the heavens seemed to open like a floodgate and hurl more water than the earth had ever seen down upon those barren paddocks north of Melbourne. Both branches of the creek had burst their banks, the footbridge to the access road had long ago been swept away; each morning I slapped more mud and rubble onto the retaining wall around my shack to keep the waters at bay and three times daily I emptied the saucepans and placed them again below the leaks in the roof. I wrote—what else could I do? The one thing I'd felt to be missing from my archaeological records, the glue that would bind the whole thing together, had suddenly been served up to me on a cold stainless steel slab. I'd brought back a lock of her hair and kept it beside me on the table; that was all I needed, whatever little gaps remained in the tale I could fill with fantasy and fiction. I wrote, a sensible story for the edification of generations to come, the story of the housing estate north of Melbourne, the people who lived there, and the sorry circumstances that led to its destruction, abandonment and ruin. I tried to keep it simple; if I wandered too far off the track I would pick up one of the objects from my table—a piece of amber glass from a broken beer bottle, a brown house brick or a charred rabbit bone—and finger it gently for a while until the direction of my story became clear to me again and I could bend down low into the yellow pool of lamplight and let my pen once more run swiftly, without thinking, across the page. The drumming of the rain on the roof was my constant companion. I ate frugally from the little food I had stored and drank from the saucepans to quench my thirst. I was happy, indescribably happy; I had witnessed the most monstrous tragedies, savage humiliations, pointless deaths, but at last it all made *sense*.

As the rain finally began to ease I had only one last section to write before the story of *ur* would be complete; then I would take all the objects I'd unearthed and bury them back in the hill. The days began to break blue and sunny, a few clouds scudded past high above, the waters slowly receded, I emptied the saucepans for the last time and put them away in the cupboard. One clear morning I pulled on my gumboots and trudged through the mud to the top of the hill. All around, smooth lakes of water lay glistening on the paddocks, the huge swathe of dirt below me was now a muddy dam. Then out on the access road I saw a car pull up. Patterson got out, went around to the back and opened the boot. I saw him climbing into a pair of green fisherman's waders, snapping the straps shut, then out of the boot he began dragging a tangle of barbed wire and broken wood. He tucked a cardboard box under one arm, dragged the canoe behind him with the other and started out across the paddocks east of the moat. He saw me watching him from the top of the hill, called out something and pointed towards my shack.

I cleared the things from my table and Patterson emptied the cardboard box onto it. He'd brought me supplies, canned food mostly, and a few cold cans of beer. The broken canoe lay in a tangled heap outside the front door. We've finished our investigations, he said, and recorded it as death by misadventure. The canoe was supposed to go to the tip but I thought you might like to have it. He reached into the breast pocket of his waders—And this—and drew out the old matted rabbit-skin hat. The hat lay on the table between us, exuding a damp animal smell, as we drank our beer in silence. Finally Patterson found the courage to speak. We found the baby, out on Huntington's back paddock, he said: there was no hope of it surviving. I got up from the table, turned to the window and looked out at the rain-drenched paddocks beyond the creek. I saw the scene: Huntington, probably a craggy-faced old farmer with a stooped-back walk, rising from his bed on the third clear day when the floods that had swept across his paddocks were finally beginning to recede, pulling on his gumboots and walking out into the still, damp air to check his fences and animals on the far side of his farm. And there, over the creek, in the back paddock where muddy puddles still dotted the ground, he saw a herd of cows standing strangely in a circle, their heads hung low, still and silent. He called them up; one by one they peeled away from the circle, revealing in its centre a tiny blue-grey bundle of flesh lying on the ground, stark and unmistakable against the background of sodden grass. Patterson woke me from my reverie. I had a message from Tony, the bricklayer, he said: he'd heard about Jodie's death. Work has started on that new housing development near Haranhope. He's offering you a job, if you want it. Perhaps you should take him up. I wanted to turn, say: No, I've got other work to do, can't you see all these things lying about, the papers stacked up in the corner? I don't want to lay bricks in Haranhope. But it sounded so stupid, and I continued gazing out the window in silence.

Patterson left; I watched him cross the muddy paddocks and the moat in his waders back to his car on the access road. I dragged the broken canoe inside and shoved it into a corner. I warmed up a can of baked beans in a saucepan while I put the rest of the food away in the cupboard and arranged my papers on the table again. I opened a can, ate my beans and sipped my beer slowly as I stared at the tangle of barbed wire and broken wood in the corner. I carefully selected a few objects from the floor and arranged them around the rabbit-skin hat. I did nothing then, for a long time, but sit and sip my beer. Evening fell, I lit the lamp. I washed out my saucepan and plate. Cows were lowing out on the paddock—so long since I'd heard that sound! The silence and stillness after a month of rain was palpable, cloying. I had only one last section to do for my story to be complete and should not have spent so much time in girding my loins for the task. But what if I botched it, now, at the end, just when all the pieces seemed to have fitted together? Finally, around midnight, the command I'd been waiting for came to me, suddenly, as if from somewhere else. To hell with it anyway! I heard my mind saying; who but you will ever know if the story rings true or not? And if you don't, if in the end even *you* never know—to hell with that too!—the oil in the lamp is almost spent.

She came that night, the darkest night, a night of no moon and torrential rain. Across the sodden paddocks she came, dragging her home-made canoe. She'd built it back at camp, in the weeks following Michael's arrest, ripping the wire and bits of timber from the tumbledown fences around her and piecing it together from the sketches she carried, her hands all scratched and torn. Each night she read the instructions and waited for the moon to wane. And then, on that night, a night with no moon, she dragged it across the paddocks towards the old ruins of *ur*. She crossed the freeway, well to the south, then journeyed north-east and crossed the access road too. She stopped then, and thought for a moment of wheeling around across the paddocks to the shack she could now just make out in the distance through a sheet of driving rain, a thin plume of smoke rising from its chimney. But instead—her reasons were her own—she continued north, over the old tip site, to the edge of the swollen creek. She pushed the bow of the canoe into the water and with the jar of salt in her hand she stepped gingerly inside. But hardly had she gained her footing than the current grabbed it and began to carry it swiftly downstream. She struggled to stay upright as the canoe turned around and around in maddening circles, bow first, then stern, then bow then stern again. She steadied herself with one hand on the bulwark, the barbed wire ripping her flesh, as with the jar in the other hand she tried to bail out the rising bilge. Past Vito's old vegetable garden, the junction of the moat and the scattered ruins of North-East Court, the canoe drifted and spun, sinking ever-lower in the water. I'd have been at my table, my back to the window, when it passed by almost sunk in the swollen creek at the far end of my garden. Did I hear her feeble Help!, cried out as instructed? No, I don't think so. I was watching the fragments of my story fly up from my table like so many startled starlings from a tree. I was saying; sleep now, dream, and in a dream the idea may come that will bring them all back to roost. The rain fell hard and unending on the roof. All the ghosts of *ur* were sleeping. The night was as dark as a whale's belly. She passed by swiftly, cried out softly; I wasn't listening, I couldn't have heard.

The skies have cleared, the lakes and puddles out on the paddocks have drained away and dried, the creek trickles past at the end of the garden, returned to its former size. Though the fertile silt washed up all around looks like a gardener's dream, I haven't bothered to replant my vegetables nor do any of the things I had planned to do when the weather finally cleared. The smell of the earth after so much rain is a strange and intoxicating thing; I've been content most days just to stand at my door and draw it languorously into my nostrils. Since the rain stopped and my story was finished I've done very little else, though I've managed to re-bury most of the junk I'd collected back in the hole in the hill. That took me a week, in a slow-moving dream; I barely had the strength to lift the shovel. For three days I anguished over what to do with the tangle of barbed wire in the corner; in the end I dumped it unceremoniously back into the creek. Most of the things in the house are packed, my bundle of papers in a cardboard box. Today I went to the top of the hill to take one last look over old *ur* and saw the bulldozers trundling towards me in the distance. The freeway was coming again. It will be a sharp turn to head west from here, I thought, and in the years to come the drivers encountering it on their way to Haranhope will mutter a low curse at such shoddy planning. And yes, in the end old *ur* will perhaps only be remembered as a dangerous bend in the freeway north of Melbourne, just where it crosses a dry creek bed before turning sharply left towards the new estate in the west. Patterson arrived in the afternoon—his last benevolent gesture—to help tow my car from the bog. I spent the remaining daylight hours packing the last of my things. There was little to do then but sit and think—it's a pleasant pastime, that. About Michael, Jodie, my neighbours, all gone, and the sometimes silly things that happen in this life and that so soon pass into the obscurity of history. It was only an experiment, I thought, built too far out in the wrong direction, favoured or flawed by its own possibility. Should someone dig it all up again one day I'm sure they'd make a damned sight more sense of it than me. I had my bundle of papers, certainly, and sometime, somewhere, on an evening like this, they might bring me a little comfort and take the sting out of that day's particular disillusionment. But I would not be setting sail on them, hat on head and jar in hand. No, that nonsense is over, my days here are done, tomorrow I leave for Haranhope where a barrow of bricks lies waiting. This time I'll start from the bottom up and see what comes of that.